Dear Reader,

We're thrilled that some of Harlequin's most famous families are making an encore appearance! With this special Famous Families fifty-book collection, we are proud to offer you the chance to relive the drama, the glamour, the suspense and the romance of four of Harlequin's most beloved families—the Fortunes, the Bravos, the McCabes and the Cavanaughs.

You'll begin your journey at the Double Crown ranch in Red Rock, Texas, home of the legendary Fortunes and the setting of the twelve-book miniseries Fortunes of Texas: Reunion. Members of the family are preparing to honor their patriarch, Ryan Fortune, but a bloodred moon offers a portent of trouble ahead. As the clan deals with a mysterious body, an abduction, a health crisis and numerous family secrets, each member also manages to find love and a happily-ever-after you'll want to share.

We hope you enjoy your time in Red Rock. Be prepared for our next stop, the Rising Sun Ranch in Medicine Creek, Wyoming, where USA TODAY bestselling author Christine Rimmer kicks off the story of the Bravo family. Watch for The Nine-Month Marriage, the first of the Bravo series, beginning in March!

Happy reading,

The Editors

PEGGY MORELAND

published her first romance with Silhouette Books in 1989 and continues to delight readers with stories set in her home state of Texas. Peggy is a winner of a National Readers' Choice Award, a nominee for an *RT Book Reviews* Reviewer's Choice Award and a two-time finalist for a prestigious RITA® Award. Her books also frequently appear on the *USA TODAY* and Waldenbooks' bestseller lists. When not writing, Peggy can usually be found outside, tending the cattle, goats and other critters on the ranch she shares with her husband.

FAMOUS FAMILIES

the FORTUNES

USA TODAY Bestselling Author

PEGGY MORELAND

In the Arms of the Law

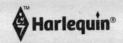

Harlequin®

TORONTO NEW YORK LONDON
AMSTERDAM PARIS SYDNEY HAMBURG
STOCKHOLM ATHENS TOKYO MILAN MADRID
PRAGUE WARSAW BUDAPEST AUCKLAND

Special thanks and acknowledgment
are given to Peggy Moreland for her contribution
to the Fortunes of Texas: Reunion series.

Recycling programs
for this product may
not exist in your area.

ISBN-13: 978-0-373-36482-4

IN THE ARMS OF THE LAW

FAMOUS FAMILIES

The Fortunes

Cowboy at Midnight by Ann Major
A Baby Changes Everything by Marie Ferrarella
In the Arms of the Law by Peggy Moreland
Lone Star Rancher by Laurie Paige
The Good Doctor by Karen Rose Smith
The Debutante by Elizabeth Bevarly
Keeping Her Safe by Myrna Mackenzie
The Law of Attraction by Kristi Gold
Once a Rebel by Sheri WhiteFeather
Military Man by Marie Ferrarella
Fortune's Legacy by Maureen Child
The Reckoning by Christie Ridgway

The Bravos by Christine Rimmer

The Nine-Month Marriage
Marriage by Necessity
Practically Married
Married by Accident
The Millionaire She Married
The M.D. She Had to Marry
The Marriage Agreement
The Bravo Billionaire
The Marriage Conspiracy
His Executive Sweetheart
Mercury Rising
Scrooge and the Single Girl

The McCabes by Cathy Gillen Thacker

Dr. Cowboy
Wildcat Cowboy
A Cowboy's Woman
A Cowboy Kind of Daddy
A Night Worth Remembering
The Seven-Year Proposal
The Dad Next Door
The Last Virgin in Texas
Texas Vows: A McCabe Family Saga
The Ultimate Texas Bachelor
Santa's Texas Lullaby
A Texas Wedding Vow
Blame It on Texas
A Laramie, Texas Christmas
From Texas, With Love

The Cavanaughs by Marie Ferrarella

Racing Against Time
Crime and Passion
Internal Affair
Dangerous Games
The Strong Silent Type
Cavanaugh's Woman
In Broad Daylight
Alone in the Dark
Dangerous Disguise
The Woman Who Wasn't There
Cavanaugh Watch
Cavanaugh Heat

Prologue

The glare of the midday sun and lack of wind had turned Lake Mondo into a mirror, its surface reflecting the cedars and outcropping of rocks that lined its shore. A long wooden dock—bleached a dull gray by weather and time—stretched out over the water and bobbed lazily in the slow-moving current. On any other day, swimmers and fishermen alike would be vying for position on the planked walkway, as well as along the lake's shore. But today both the dock and the shoreline were empty...except for the lone body lying faceup beneath a white sheet.

Yellow crime-scene tape sectioned off a large

portion of the area surrounding the dock, holding back the curious and morbid who had gathered. The few officials allowed beyond the tape huddled in a loose group, their expressions grim, as they watched the police photographer digitally record the scene.

Quickly assessing the area as she approached, Detective Andrea Matthews ducked beneath the tape and headed straight for the body. The stench that grew stronger with each step was her first clue that this wasn't a recent drowning.

In her peripheral vision, she caught a glimpse of Red Rock Police Officer Gabe Thunderhawk breaking away from the group and heading her way. She swallowed a groan when he stopped in front of her and braced his hands on his hips, successfully blocking her progress, as well as her view of the corpse. Since he had about five inches on her five foot seven inch frame, she was forced to look up at him, a form of intimidation she was sure he intended. Though he was as handsome as the devil himself and a lot easier to look at than a corpse, she had a job to do and wasn't interested in getting into a verbal sparring match over who was in charge of this investigation, which was what she figured he had in mind.

Hoping to avoid an altercation, she lifted her chin, indicating the body behind him. "Looks like we've got ourselves a floater."

He glanced over his shoulder, then returned his gaze to hers. "Good deduction, Detective."

Though his expression remained bland, his sarcasm set her teeth on edge. Rather than respond to it, she stepped around him, planning to ignore him.

He quickly shifted to block her way. "No need for you to concern yourself with this one. I've got everything under control."

At the end of her patience, she squared off with him. "You know damn good and well that when there's a body involved, it's my job to investigate it. Now, you can either assist in the investigation or get the hell out of my way, because I intend to do my job, with or without your cooperation."

He met her gaze a full ten seconds, making her think he was going to force the issue, but finally stepped aside.

Pulling a mask from her blazer pocket, she nodded to the police photographer, before slipping it over her head to cover her nose and mouth. With her gaze on the body, she tugged on a pair of protective gloves and hunkered down beside it. Careful not to disturb any evidence, she lifted the sheet to expose the victim's face. Finding him lying face-down, she dropped the sheet back over him.

"Help me turn him over," she instructed Gabe.

Keeping the cover in place, they worked together to roll the victim to his back, then Andrea lifted the sheet again. Although this wasn't the first drowning she'd investigated, she had to swallow back the nausea that burned the back of her throat. Blank eyes stared up at her from a bloated and distorted face. The victim's skin, blanched a sickly blue-white, was pitted where bits of flesh were missing, probably due to predators he'd encountered during the time he'd spent in the water.

There was also what appeared to be a bullet hole between his eyes.

Aware that Gabe was watching for her reaction, she set her jaw and dropped the sheet back over the victim's face. Pulling the mask down, she stood to face the officer. "So what have you got?"

"Nine-one-one call came in about an hour ago. Placed by the fishing guide who found the body. The guy's sitting in the backseat of my patrol car. Still pretty shook up."

She nodded grimly. "I would imagine he is." Frowning, she circled the body, examining it from different angles. "Any ID?"

"Checked his pockets. No wallet or any kind of ID, although I did notice what appears to be a birthmark on his hip. Looks like we've got a John Doe."

"The M.E.'s report will detail any identifying marks." She stopped and hunkered down beside the body again, lifting the sheet away from the lower extremities. "He wasn't dressed for fishing or swimming," she commented, noting the slacks he wore.

"Judging by the three holes in his head, I'd say his visit to the lake wasn't recreational."

She snapped her gaze up to Gabe's, her brows drawn together in question. "Three?"

"Bullet entered here, here and here," he said, indicating each by pointing them out on his own head. "I'm no expert, but I'd say he was dead before he hit the water."

Irritated with herself that he'd found three bullet holes, when she'd only seen one, she looked at the corpse again. Her frown deepening, she slowly lowered the sheet and pushed to her feet. "Has the M.E. been here?"

"Here and gone about half an hour ago. Left as soon as he proclaimed him dead. When the photographer finishes up, we're transporting the body to the lab for autopsy."

Andrea nodded. "I'll drop by and get the M.E.'s preliminary findings."

"I plan on doing the same. Want a ride? We can have dinner afterward."

She rolled her eyes. "Do you ever give up, Thunderhawk?"

"Do I look like a quitter?"

"Are we ready to transport?"

Startled by the sound of Chief Prater's voice, she glanced over her shoulder and saw that he was headed their way. As usual, he had an unlit cigar clamped between his teeth. Although he'd quit smoking five years before, he refused to give up his cigars completely.

"We're transporting as soon as the photographer finishes up," she replied, then looked at him curiously. "What are you doing way out here? You don't usually visit crime scenes."

"Got a call from the M.E. He says our victim has an unusual birthmark. A crown shape on the right hip, same as Ryan Fortune."

Familiar with the wealthy Fortune and his philanthropic work to many of the charitable organizations in the state, Andi glanced back at the body in confusion. "Are you saying the floater is Ryan Fortune?"

"No, I'm saying the crown-shaped birthmark is a Fortune trademark, which means he's probably related." He shifted his gaze to Gabe. "I want you working this case with Andi."

Andi's eyes shot wide in alarm. "Leo and I can handle this. We don't need Gabe's help."

The chief dragged the cigar from his mouth and set his lips in a grim line. "Leo isn't going to be handling anything for a while."

A knot of fear twisted in her gut. "But...why? Has something happened to him?"

He tapped a finger against his chest. "Heart attack. Happened early this morning. His wife says it was caused by a blockage. Gonna need a quadruple bypass. He'll be out on medical leave for at least a month. Maybe longer."

Stunned, Andi could only stare at her boss, her concern for her partner obliterating all other thought. She'd worked with Leo for nine years. Heck, he was like a father to her!

She swallowed hard, trying to force back the paralyzing fear, the memory of her own father's heart attack that had resulted in his death.

"He's going to be okay, isn't he?" she asked uneasily.

The chief shrugged. "If he takes care of himself and follows the doctor's orders, he should be fine." He narrowed an eye at her. "But until he's back, Gabe's working with you. Understood?"

Though Andi wanted to argue, beg the chief to assign someone else as her partner, anyone other than Thunderhawk, she gave her chin a jerk of assent. "Whatever you say, Chief."

He clamped the unlit cigar between his teeth again and took a slow look around. "Looks like y'all've done what you can do here. Go on over to Ryan's ranch, inform him of what's happened, then escort him to the M.E.'s office and see if he can identify the body."

"Do you really think our floater is a Fortune?" she asked doubtfully.

He looked down his nose at her. "Until someone proves otherwise, that's exactly what I think."

Chapter 1

Two months later

Andi Matthews was no stranger to murder. She'd focused her entire college career on studying the profiles of killers and perfecting the procedures for gathering the evidence needed to win convictions. For the past nine years she'd worked for the Red Rock Police Department, had personally investigated close to fifty murders and put nearly that same number of criminals behind bars. She knew how a murderer's mind worked, what fueled their need to kill and what mistakes they might make that would lead to their arrests.

But she'd never considered committing murder herself.

Until today.

From the moment Chief Prater had assigned Gabe Thunderhawk to work with her to identify the body of the Lost Fortune—the tag given to the floater discovered at Lake Mondo—she'd known she was in for trouble. Everyone on the force knew that Gabe wanted a promotion to detective, and this was the perfect chance for him to prove he was qualified to handle the job.

Intellectually she understood what a boon the successful closing of the case would be to his career. Because of the crown-shaped birthmark on the floater's right hip that linked the body with the Fortune family, solving the case would give him a level of publicity and notoriety that no other case could offer.

But understanding his motive in no way excused his behavior. Not in Andi's opinion. *She* was the primary on this case and she was sick and tired of him working independently from her. They were supposed to be partners, a team, a fact that she intended to remind him of the moment he showed up…if he ever did.

She stopped her agitated pacing in front of the police station and shoved up the sleeve of her blazer to check the time. Her frown deepened, as she noted that he was now over thirty minutes late.

"Okay, Thunderhawk," she muttered under her breath. "What are you up to now?"

While playing the possibilities through her mind, she recalled mentioning the day before that they should requestion the fishing guide who had found the body. Figuring Gabe had taken it upon himself to do the job alone—and upstaging her should he get lucky—she headed for her unmarked, city-issue Ford sedan.

The twenty-minute drive to Lake Mondo gave her ample time to work up a pretty good head of steam. By the time she arrived at Hook 'n Go, the bait shop where the fishing guide usually hung out, and found Gabe's truck parked out front, she was a slash mark beyond the boiling point. Prepared to read him the riot act for his traitorous behavior the moment he showed his double-crossing face, she braced a hip against the hood of his truck, folded her arms across her chest and waited.

Her timing was perfect, as moments later the door of the bait shop opened and Gabe appeared. Seemingly unaware of her presence, he paused in the doorway, conversing with someone inside. He didn't appear rushed or harried, a fact that grated on her already raw nerves, since he'd kept her cooling her heels for almost an hour. But Gabe never seemed to get in a hurry, a trait the guys on the force attributed to his Native American heritage. That same heritage was evidenced by his high slash of cheekbones, the bronze tint of his skin, his dark hair and eyes. Most women considered him drop-dead handsome. Normally Andi would've agreed.

Today she considered him nothing but a royal pain in the ass.

"I appreciate your time," she heard him say to the person inside. "If you think of anything, you've got my card." The slap of the screen door closing was followed by the scrape of his boot soles on the worn wooden steps as he headed for his truck.

When he spotted Andi, he slowed slightly, then strode on, his brow wrinkled in puzzlement.

"What are you doing here?" he asked. "I thought we were supposed to meet at the station."

"Oh, we were," she replied, then pushed away from his truck, with a scowl, and leveled a warning finger at his nose. "Listen up, Thunderhawk, and listen good. Whether you like it or not, I'm the primary on this investigation, and nothing is done outside of my presence or without my prior knowledge, including interviewing individuals associated with this case."

He held up a hand. "Now, wait a minute. You're the one who said we should talk to the fishing guide again."

"Yes, I did. But *we* didn't talk to him, *you* did, and after being told repeatedly that we work as a team." She narrowed an eye. "I'm warning you, Gabe, if you continue to undermine my authority,

I'll request that Chief Prater remove you from the case."

He hitched his hands on his hips in frustration. "What is it with you, anyway? You act like I'm sneaking around behind your back."

"Well, aren't you?"

"What I was trying to do was save us both some time."

"And how did you plan to do that, when I've been sitting on my hands at the station for over an hour waiting for you?"

"My place is a couple of miles from here. I figured I'd stop by on my way into town, question the guide, then meet you at the station and report my findings. Is it my fault the fishing guide is a Chatty Cathy?"

Though his explanation made sense, she didn't trust him. Not for a minute. This wasn't the first time he'd struck out on his own without first discussing his plans with her. But to continue to debate his insubordination would be unproductive and a waste of more of her time.

She released a breath and, along with it, some of her anger. "All right," she said, grudgingly. "But next time check with me first or I swear I'll file a complaint with the chief."

"Fine."

Determined to focus her mind on the investigation and away from her irritation with her so-called partner, she asked, "Did the guide have anything new to say?"

He lifted a shoulder. "Same story he gave the day he found the body."

She hadn't expected the man would remember anything new. But after two months with no new leads on the case, there was nothing left to do but backtrack, in hopes of finding something they'd missed the first time through.

Frustrated by the lack of evidence they had to work with, she frowned at the lake that had regurgitated the Lost Fortune, washing its bloated body up on shore. Thanks to the southeasterly wind currently blowing, the lake's surface was choppy. Not a fishing or pleasure boat in sight. A lone heron sailed low over the water, trolling for his next meal. The shoreline itself was empty of humanity, but dotted with litter. Aluminum cans, plastic bags and a length of frayed synthetic rope, probably discarded from some ski boat. It was a scavenger's dream.

As she watched a wave wash the litter higher onto shore, an idea began to grow in her mind.

"What was the weather like the day before the body was discovered?"

He gave her an impatient look. "How the hell would I know?"

"If we can find out which direction the wind was

blowing prior to the body being found, we might be able to pinpoint the area where it was dumped."

"Yeah," he said dryly, "and if we had a crystal ball we could probably look inside and see who dumped it."

She burned him with a look. "Do you have a better idea?"

He turned and walked away.

"Where are you going?" she asked in frustration.

"Inside," he called over his shoulder. "Ten-to-one the owner of the bait shop keeps a weather journal."

Kicking herself for not having thought of that herself, she watched Gabe walk toward the bait house—and wished she'd kept her eyes on the lake. Seeing his backside reminded her of the discussion she'd overheard in the women's restroom that morning. Several of the female employees had decided that Gabe deserved the "Cutest Butt on the Force" award. She let her gaze slide to his hips. Even though she hadn't offered a comment on the subject, she had to agree. He did have a fine-looking tush.

Unfortunately, his butt wasn't his only outstanding feature. Wide shoulders; slim waist; muscled chest, arms and legs. He was the only man she knew who could make a department-issue khaki uniform look as if it was custom-tailored for him by Armani.

Too bad he'd let his physical attributes go to

his head. He had an ego the size of Texas and was a playboy to boot. Two traits that, in her mind at least, nullified his finer points.

With a sigh, she turned her gaze to the lake and waited. To pass the time she counted the waves that rushed onto shore.

"Wind was from the northwest," Gabe reported moments later as he rejoined her. "Gusts up to seventy-two miles per hour."

She glanced at the sun, seeking a point of reference, then across the span of white-capped water toward the northwest quadrant of the lake. "Do you know what's over there?"

"A few private homes, a public boat ramp and acres of undeveloped land."

"I say we start with the public ramp," she said and turned for her car.

He fell into step beside her. "We can take my truck."

"No way. I value my life too much to climb into a vehicle with you behind the wheel."

"Hey," he said, sounding insulted. "There's nothing wrong with my driving." He stopped at the side of his truck and opened the passenger door. "Besides, my truck's got four-wheel drive. Depending on how far you want to explore, we might need it."

She hesitated a moment, considering, then heaved a sigh and climbed inside, knowing he was right.

"No speeding," she warned as he slid behind the wheel. "And none of those fancy one-eighties they teach at the police academy."

He put the truck in gear, shot her a grin, then spun the wheel and stomped on the accelerator. With a squeal of tires, they were headed in the opposite direction. Andi grabbed for the chicken bar above the passenger window and hung on, silently vowing to kill him later.

By the time they reached the turnoff for the boat ramp, her knuckles were white and her feet burned from pressing the imaginary brake on the floorboard. Thankfully, the road that led to the ramp was full of potholes, which forced him to slow down. It was also bordered by shoulder-high weeds and even taller cedars, the perfect cover for someone who had something—or someone—to hide. As they neared the lake, the road widened, with parking space available to both sides of a long, weathered dock.

As soon as he pulled to a stop, Andi opened her door and jumped to the ground. "Next time I drive," she muttered irritably.

Gabe met her at the hood. "You shouldn't have said anything about my driving. It was like a dare." He lifted a brow and looked down his nose at her. "And I've never been able to walk away from a dare."

"I'll remember that in the future," she said dryly,

then pushed up her sleeves, eager to get to work. "Okay. Here's how we're going to play this. We'll assume that the murder took place somewhere other than at the lake."

"Any particular reason?"

"Mainly because none of the residents who live around the lake reported hearing gunshots."

"He could have used a silencer."

"True, but my gut tells me the murder took place somewhere else and the killer used the lake as a depository, hoping the body would never be discovered."

He lifted a shoulder. "You're the boss."

"We're also going to assume that the murderer dumped the body at night. Otherwise, he'd risk being seen."

"I can buy that," he agreed.

She stepped to the edge of the water and frowned as she studied the moss-covered concrete ramp that stretched beyond the surface. "So what would he do?" she asked, thinking aloud, as she tried to slip into the mind of the perp. "Back his vehicle to the edge, as if he was going to put a boat into the water, then dump the body?" She cut her gaze to the pier. "Or would he carry it onto the dock and drop it over the side?"

"Depends on his physical condition. If our perp is in good shape, he'd probably carry the body to the end of the dock. The water's deeper there. It would also save him from getting wet."

She nodded her agreement.

"There's also the possibility that he used a boat," he reminded her. "He could have concealed the body in the hull prior to driving to the lake, put in here at the ramp, then shoved the body overboard once he was far enough away from the shoreline to avoid detection."

"Yes, but we've already checked with the owners of the boats known to be on the water that night. Each was aware of the others' presence and all agreed that theirs were the only boats on the lake. All three owners were questioned individually and their stories matched."

"Then we go with the theory that the murderer dumped the body from the dock or shore."

"For now." She turned away. "You check the shoreline. I'll take the dock."

"Wait a minute," he said, stopping her. "Any evidence left behind would've washed away or been destroyed by now."

"Maybe we'll get lucky."

Though she could tell by his expression that he considered the search a waste of time, he didn't offer any more arguments. Surprised that he was cooperating with her for a change, she headed for the dock.

As she stepped onto the weathered surface, the

barrels that supported it pitched beneath her weight. She gave herself a moment to adjust to the rolling movement, then walked slowly to the opposite end, casting her gaze from side to side. Long strands of slimy-looking vegetation swayed beneath the surface of the murky water, tugged by the current. She stifled a shudder. She loved swimming, but preferred man-made pools with concrete bottoms and chlorine-treated water over lakes, with all their aquatic vegetation and muddy base.

At the end of the dock, she squatted down and looked over the edge, trying to imagine the murderer's movements if he'd chosen this particular method to dispose of the body. Several feet beneath the water's surface, she caught a glimpse of a scrap of fabric snagged on one of the support posts.

Though she knew the chances of the fabric being torn from Lost Fortune's clothing were slim, she pushed up a sleeve and reached to retrieve it. Just short of touching the water, she jerked her hand back to fist against her thigh. She gulped as she stared into the murky water. She wasn't a sissy. Not by any stretch of the imagination. But she had a deathly fear of snakes, and water moccasins, one of Texas's most poisonous snakes, made their homes in lakes and ponds.

Catching her lower lip between her teeth, she glanced Gabe's way, thinking she'd ask him to retrieve the piece of cloth.

But if she did, she knew she would be exposing her fear of snakes and setting herself up to be on the receiving end of practical jokes from not only Gabe, but every guy on the force. Rubber snakes in her desk. Curled on the seat of her car. Stuffed into her mail slot. The possibilities were endless.

With a sigh of resignation, she shrugged off her blazer, leaving her arms bare, then drew in a deep breath and thrust her hand into the water. She shuddered in revulsion as long strands of weeds brushed against her fingers and wound around her arm. The colorful bit of fabric swayed inches from her fingertips, and she leaned farther over, straining to reach it.

"Just a little bit more," she encouraged under her breath.

She heard a sharp popping sound and, at the same moment, felt the plank beneath her right knee give way. She only had time to draw in one shocked breath before the board broke and she was pitched headfirst into the water.

As she plunged downward, vegetation grabbed at her and slapped at her face. In her mind, each tendril was a snake, slithering over her skin. She wanted to scream, but the thought of swallowing even a teaspoon of the vile water kept the sound lodged in her throat.

Fear had her kicking hard and fighting her way back to the top. As she broke through the surface, she released the scream that burned in her throat. Sobbing, she clawed at the slime that clung to her arms and chest, while trying to remain afloat.

Something hard and flat slammed against the top of her head—a pressure she realized was Gabe's hand a split second before he shoved her down under the water. She came up sputtering and slapping at him, blinded by the water in her eyes.

"Andi!" he shouted. "Relax! I've got you."

Before she could tell him she wasn't drowning, he hooked an arm beneath her chin and began to drag her toward shore. Once on the bank, he released her, dumping her unceremoniously in the mud and moss on the concrete boat ramp.

He dropped down next to her and blew out a long breath. "Lucky thing I was here," he said. "Otherwise you might've drowned."

Sprawled in mud and slime, she pushed up to her elbows and scowled at his back. "I wasn't drowning, you idiot."

He glanced over his shoulder. "Then why the scream?"

Embarrassed that he'd heard that, she sat up and brushed at the weeds that clung to her slacks, avoiding his gaze. "I'm scared of snakes," she admitted reluctantly.

He stared a moment, then hooted a laugh. "Hell, if there was a snake within a mile of you,

you would've scared it away with all that flapping around you were doing."

"Oh, right," she snapped irritably. "I forget. You're an Indian. You probably would've killed it with your tomahawk and made a headband or something out of its skin."

She knew immediately by the stiffening of his shoulders that she'd said the wrong thing.

"I'm sorry," she said with real regret. "I didn't mean that."

He pushed to his feet. "We better get out of these wet clothes."

"Gabe, really. It was a stupid thing to say. I was just mad because I fell in the lake, and I took it out on you."

"Forget it." He offered her a hand. "Come on. Let's go to my place and get cleaned up. I've got a washer and dryer."

Though she'd have preferred a long soak in her own tub, the thought of the thirty-odd-minute drive back to town in muddy clothes made her reconsider. "All right," she agreed and allowed him to pull her to her feet. "But I'm getting that piece of fabric off the post before I go anywhere."

"I'll get it."

She knew she should insist upon retrieving it herself, to prove to him she wasn't a coward. But the thought of going anywhere near that pier kept her lips sealed tight.

She watched him drop down on his stomach at the end of the pier and reach into the water. "Can you tell what it is?" she called as he pulled his arm out.

He stood and lifted the scrap of fabric for her to see. "Orange canvas from a life preserver. Judging by its rotted state, I'd say it's been here for years."

Her shoulders sagged in disappointment.

Another dead end.

Gabe seldom brought women to his house—and it wasn't because he was ashamed of the place. The cedar-framed cabin might be rustic in design, but it had every modern convenience the tract homes in town offered, plus a few. It was owned by an elderly politician from Austin, who had used the place to entertain constituents and fellow legislators. Now that his failing health had bound him to a wheelchair, he no longer had need for the place and had leased it to Gabe. Since the deal they'd cut had included fishing rights to the lake on the property and hunting rights on the three thousand acres surrounding it, the cabin suited Gabe just fine.

But as he pulled out a pair of sweat pants and a T-shirt for Andi to wear while her clothes were washed, he found himself wondering what she thought of his home. He snorted a breath, remembering her remark about his Indian heritage. Hell, she was probably relieved to discover that he didn't live in a teepee!

He gave his head a woeful shake. Ordinarily comments about his heritage didn't bother him, but for some reason Andi's had stung. Maybe it was because he wanted and needed her approval so badly. He had a strong feeling that she was one of the reasons he hadn't made detective yet, and he'd hoped that by working with her on this case he could win her endorsement.

Or maybe it was because he had a serious case of the hots for her.

He choked a laugh. Yeah, like he had a snowball's chance in hell of scoring with Detective Andrea Matthews. Though he'd prefer to blame department policy on her refusal to go out with him, Andi lived by her own set of rules. From day one, she'd made it clear to every single guy on the force—fellow sufferers with Gabe, who'd like nothing better than to get in the detective's pants—that she didn't date co-workers.

But Gabe wasn't a man to give up easily.

She had become a challenge to him...and an attractive one at that. Triweekly workouts at the gym kept her body firm and toned. And she had the most gorgeous mane of curly brown hair she insisted on hiding by twisting it into a bun on top of her head or pulling it back into a ponytail. He'd imagined himself freeing that wild mass of hair, knotting his fingers in it and kissing her senseless, until she was putty in his hands.

He shoved a knee against the dresser drawer, closing it. Not a bad fantasy for a man to savor while out fishing alone or waiting for sleep to take him at night, he told himself.

But if fantasizing about her distracted him from his fishing or kept him awake too long, all he had to do was remind himself of her faults. She had a tendency to speak her mind, which bugged the hell out of him. And her tomboy reputation around the station certainly couldn't be considered an asset. Not to a man who preferred his women soft, feminine and willing.

But lately he'd begun to suspect that beneath that tomboyish facade lay a sensual woman. It would simply take the right man to peel off the layers to reveal her.

And he figured he was just the man for the job.

So far he was batting zero, but patience was one of his strongest virtues—although the lady was definitely putting a strain on it. She stiff-armed anyone who tried to get too close. The only two people on the force who could claim any type of relationship with her were her partner Leo, an overweight, grouchy old man with thinning hair, who happened to be married, and Deirdre, a female officer with whom Gabe had shared a brief and regrettable fling.

Which was Deirdre's fault, he thought, silently absolving himself of any guilt over the end of his relationship with her. She was the one who had turned what he'd hoped would be a sexually satisfying relationship into a nightmare, thanks to her possessiveness. And if she didn't ease up on the harassing phone calls and quit tailing him around town, he was going to add stalker to that list.

"Gabe?"

Startled by the sound of Andi's voice, he snapped his head around and found her peeking through a narrow crack in the bathroom door. That mass of wild, curly hair he enjoyed fantasizing about was tamed now by water and hung well past her shoulders in wet, dark tendrils. He could see just enough of the rest of her body to know that she was wearing nothing but a towel, evidenced by the swell of flesh above the terry fabric that bound her chest and the length of bare thigh visible below it. The sight was enough to make his mouth water and his groin ache.

"Did you find me something to wear?" she asked hesitantly.

He considered a moment the proximity of his bed, imagining the two of them rolling around on it, then gave himself a shake and lifted a hand, indicating the sweatpants and T-shirt he held. "Best I could do." He tossed the clothes onto the bed and turned for the door. "When you're dressed, come on down to the den. I'll fire up my computer and we can run a check on the database for missing persons."

As he jogged down the stairs, he blew out a long, slow breath, telling himself he had to possess the willpower of a monk for being able to walk away from all that bare flesh. But he had his reasons. The one conclusion he'd drawn after two months of working closely with Andi was that she preferred to be appreciated for her mind rather than her body. Personally, Gabe didn't understand why a man couldn't do both...or at least pretend to, when the ultimate reward was her body.

By the time Andi made it to the den, he had a phone tucked between shoulder and ear and had signed on to his e-mail account. Though he heard the pad of her bare feet on the wooden floor behind him, he didn't glance her way, yet another way he hoped to prove to her he had no physical designs on her.

"Drag up a chair," he told her. "I've got Reynolds on the phone. He's going to check the national database for missing persons for us."

He heard the scrape of wood against wood as she shifted a chair into position, then caught the scent of his own bath soap on her skin as she settled beside him. He had to fight the temptation to lean close and inhale the fragrance of her freshly washed hair.

He tipped the phone away from his mouth. "Reynolds says there are three new names in our region. Twenty-four nationwide. Slow day, I guess. Do you want to narrow the search first by gender or identifying marks?"

"Gender. There's always the chance that whoever filed the report failed to mention the birthmark."

He relayed the information to Reynolds, then sat back and waited, keeping the phone tucked between his shoulder and ear. Out of the corner of his eyes he saw that Andi had her arms folded over her breasts. Probably to disguise the fact that she wasn't wearing a bra. But he didn't plan for her to hold that pose for long.

After listening to Reynolds's report, he said to Andi, "That narrows it to two in our region and eleven nationwide. Want to try identifying marks or would you prefer Reynolds do an age-range search?"

"Age-range," she replied. "Same reason as before."

With a nod of confirmation, he passed the parameters of their search on to Reynolds, then sat back, mimicking her posture by folding his arms over his chest. He purposefully bumped her elbow with his in the process, and she quickly dropped her arms and shifted out of his way.

Bingo, he thought, hiding a smile. He dropped his arms to bring the receiver closer to his ear and listened to Reynolds's report. "That reduces the number to zero in our region," he told Andi, "and three nationwide."

"Tell him to pull up all three," she replied. "Let's see what information has been posted about them."

"Pull up all three," Gabe repeated to Reynolds. "Copy what's posted and shoot them to me in an e-mail, all right?"

After thanking Reynolds for his help, he disconnected the call and set the phone aside. Seconds later his computer beeped, signaling the receipt of an e-mail. Gabe quickly opened the message and began to scan it, but managed to keep one eye on Andi. She was leaning forward in her chair now, reading the message on the screen. The T-shirt he had loaned her looked more like a tent on her small frame, but he could see the slight impressions of her nipples on the fabric. Thanks to her fall into the lake and the wet shirt it had left her with, he already had a pretty good idea of the size and shape of her breasts, which he would sum up as small but firm and having dark brown centers. The thrust of her nipples against the T-shirt added yet another level of dimension to the image he'd previously filed away, one that would probably drive him crazy later that night when he was alone in his bed.

She sank back in the chair with a sigh of defeat. "Nothing."

He slung an arm around her shoulders and

hugged her against his side. "Hey. Don't look so blue. We'll identify the guy eventually."

She turned her head slowly and gave his arm a pointed look.

He lifted his hands in surrender. "Sorry. I was just trying to cheer you up."

"When I feel I need cheering up, I'll let you know." Scowling, she rose and paced away, hugging her arms over her breasts again. "How much longer before my clothes are ready?"

He bit back a smile, as he closed the screen and shut down his computer. "Twenty minutes or so. They're in the dryer now. Would you like something to eat while we wait?"

"No, but I'd take some coffee, if you have any."

"None made, but won't take me a minute to brew some."

He led the way to the kitchen, with her trailing behind.

As he measured grounds, she wandered around.

"Nice place," she said after a minute.

He lifted a shoulder. "Works for me." He switched on the coffeemaker, then turned, bracing his hips on the counter behind him. "The drive to work is a pain, but two steps out my back door is all the fishing and hunting a man could want."

Rolling her eyes, she pulled out a chair at the table and sat down. "I should've known you'd be a hunter."

"What's wrong with being a hunter?"

"It's a coward's sport! Give the animal a weapon and I'll bet you'd lose your fondness for hunting pretty darn fast."

"Assuming the animal was a good shot." Amused by the sour look she sent him, he turned and pulled two mugs from the cupboard. "But if it'll make you feel any better, I don't hunt for sport."

"There's another reason to sit in a deer blind?"

"I don't sit in a deer blind, and yes, there's another reason. Food." He placed the mugs on the table between them, then sat opposite her and stretched out his legs. "Have you ever had a venison steak?"

She snorted a breath. "No, and I'm not interested in trying one."

"You're missing a treat. Venison sausage is good, too. As for fishing," he went on, "I don't do that for the sport of it, either. I eat what I catch. There's a lake on the property, which keeps me supplied with fresh fish year round. Usually catfish and bass."

"Do you grow your own vegetables, too?"

Ignoring the sarcasm in her voice, he rose to fetch the carafe of coffee. "Some, though I don't have a garden per se. Just a few pots of tomatoes and peppers on the deck." He filled the mugs, then used one to gesture at the plants lining the sill above the kitchen sink. "And I keep a few herbs handy for cooking."

She stared, as if he'd just confessed to being a cross-dresser.

He set a mug opposite her and sat down. "What?"

She shook her head, as if to clear it. "Nothing. I just can't imagine you puttering around plants."

He rested his elbows on the table and leaned toward her. "What do you imagine me doing?"

She huffed and looked away. "I don't think about you at all."

He lifted his mug to hide his smile. "What about you? Do you have any hobbies?"

"If you're asking if I have any interests other than my work, yes, I do."

"What?"

"I happen to enjoy gardening myself."

As soon as the words were out of her mouth, she clamped her lips together, as if she'd just blurted out a closely guarded secret, which in effect she had, since he had no idea what she did when she wasn't on duty.

"What do you grow?" he asked, hoping to keep her talking.

Grimacing, she dropped her gaze and pushed her fingertip through a drop of coffee that had dripped onto the table. "Nothing fancy," she mumbled, smearing it around. "Tomatoes, onions, a few varieties of squash."

"A friend gave me some seeds for a hybrid beef-steak tomato. Lots of meat, fewer seeds. I'll give you some, if you want."

He saw the spark of interest in her eyes, before she masked it by folding her arms over her breasts and looking away. "No, thanks. It's too late in the season to plant anything now."

He searched his mind for another topic, something she might be open to discuss that would give him insight into her private life. "So how's Leo doing?"

Her expression softened immediately at the mention of her partner. "Grouchy as ever. The doctor put him on a low-cholesterol, low-fat diet. He swears they're trying to starve him to death."

"It wouldn't hurt him to miss a few meals. He's got to be a good fifty or sixty pounds overweight."

"Closer to seventy," she said, then shrugged. "His wife's been hounding him for years to lose some weight. His doctor, too. But Leo loves to eat."

"Y'all seem to be pretty tight."

She shrugged again. "We've been partners since I joined the force. Leo may have his faults, but he's a good detective. Nose like a bloodhound. Tenacity of a bulldog. Eyes like a hawk. I've learned more from him than I ever did in a classroom."

"Maybe when he gets back from his medical leave, I'll have a chance to work with him."

"When Leo returns," she informed him, "you'll

be going back to your regular duties as an officer. Remember? This is only a temporary assignment."

Though every muscle in his body stiffened in denial at the reminder, Gabe managed to keep the emotion from his face.

Lifting his coffee cup, he took a long drink, then replied with a vague, "Maybe."

Chapter 2

When Andi strode into the patrol room the next morning, Gabe wondered if she had a funeral to attend. Black skirt, black unstructured jacket, black closed-toe shoes. The only relief to her outfit was the stark white tailored blouse she wore tucked neatly into the waist of her skirt. Nothing in her choice of attire hinted at her femininity, yet she all but screamed sex as she crossed to her desk, drawing the eye of every male on duty, Gabe's included.

Rather than the all-too-familiar ponytail, on this particular morning she'd twisted her hair up into a loose knot on the crown of her head. A pencil, honed dagger-sharp, pierced the knot's center, hold-

ing it in place. He imagined himself sliding the
pencil out and letting her hair tumble down around
her slim shoulders. It was an intriguing image and
one he'd mentally played through several times
since the previous day when he'd seen her fresh
from his shower, her hair down and dripping water
onto her shoulders.

Frowning, he forced his gaze to the file he'd
been reading before she'd arrived. He had no business indulging in sexual fantasies about Andi. Not
when she stood between him and his chance of
making detective. A bad word from her to Chief
Prater could negatively impact his chance of promotion.

And why waste his time on her, anyway? he
asked himself in frustration. She wasn't his type.
She was outspoken and bossy. What his oldest
brother Zeb would call a ballbuster.

But, damn, if his blood didn't run hot every time
he so much as looked at her.

"Thunderhawk!"

He jumped, his carnal thoughts shattered by the
chief's bellowing roar.

"Yes, sir?" he said, rising.

"In my office." The chief snatched the unlit cigar
from his mouth, and added in a kinder voice, "You,
too, Andi."

Accustomed to the chief's preferential treatment
toward his partner, Gabe closed the file he'd been

reading and headed across the room. He reached the chief's door at the same time as Andi and stepped aside, letting her enter first. His gallantry earned him a scowl.

"Sit," the chief instructed, indicating the two chairs opposite his desk. "Where are we on the McPherson case?"

Since the chief had directed the question at Andi, Gabe sat back and listened.

"We're waiting on the results from the DNA test we ordered on the rapist's semen," she told him. "McPherson won't walk this time. I can promise you that. The D.A. has assured me we've given him all he needs to win a conviction."

The chief snorted a breath. "I'll believe it when I see it. We've had that pervert up on rape charges before, and he's walked every damn time. I don't know who's slicker—him or his lawyer." Scowling, he rolled the cigar to the opposite side of his mouth and reared back in his chair. "What about the Fortune case? Anything new?"

"No, sir. We're backtracking now to see if we missed anything the first time through."

His scowl deepening, he snatched the cigar from his mouth and tossed it into the garbage can beside his desk. "I don't like having an unsolved murder on my books, and this one's been riding for over two months now."

"I don't like it any better than you do," Andi assured him. "But without a murder weapon or a witness, we have little to work with. Once we identify the floater, I'm hoping we can establish probable cause and work it from that angle."

Nodding his approval of her plan, the chief plucked a fresh cigar from the box on his desk and bit off one end. "There's a charity ball Saturday night at the country club. It's a given the Fortunes will be there. I'm going to finagle the two of you an invitation."

Andi sat up straight in her chair, obviously not pleased with the assignment. "Why? We've interviewed every Fortune in the state of Texas and not a one of them was able to identify the body."

"True," the chief agreed, "but the only clue we have is the crown-shaped birthmark on the floater's hip, and that keeps pointing us straight back to the Fortunes. Somebody in that family has to know something. I'd request DNA samples from the lot of them, but I don't want to do that until we have something more substantial to base our suspicions on. In the meantime, I want y'all at that party. Mix and mingle. See what you can find out."

He paused to run the cigar through his lips, wetting it, then shifted his gaze to Gabe. "You're going to need a tux. It's black tie."

Gabe stifled a groan. He hated wearing a tuxedo. The last one he'd worn was three years ago at his brother Matt's wedding, and he still remembered the hour-long battle he'd fought with the damn bow tie that had come with it.

"Couldn't I just wear a regular suit?" he asked, hoping to avoid the torture.

"A tux," the chief repeated sternly. "I don't want you sticking out like a sore thumb."

"There's no need for him to go to the trouble of renting a tux," Andi offered. "I can work the ball by myself."

The chief shook his head. "If you show up alone, folks might wonder what you're doing there. I don't want anyone to suspect that you're on police business."

"He's right, Andi," Gabe said, siding with the chief. "We'd draw less attention together than either of us would on our own."

Andi strode out of the chief's office, her shoulders stiff with resentment, and Gabe trailing behind.

"Why'd you have to agree with him?" she muttered irritably. "If you'd kept your mouth shut, I could've talked him into letting me go alone."

"And miss out on a chance for a date with you?"

"Hey, Andi!" a voice called from across the room. "How come you'll go on a date with Gabe and not me?"

"Stuff it, Reynolds," she growled, then flopped

down on her chair and narrowed an eye at Gabe. "And this is *not* a date."

Hiding a smile, he propped a hip on the edge of her desk. "Sure it is."

"Not in my book."

"A man and woman get all dolled up and go out for an evening at the country club?" He lifted a shoulder. "Sounds like a date to me."

She balled her hands into fists against her thighs. "It's not a date," she repeated through clenched teeth. "We're working on a case."

"Call it what you want," he said, then stood and shot her a wink. "But in my book it's a date."

She curled her lip in a snarl as he walked away, then snatched up her coffee mug and stomped from the patrol room. In the kitchen where the employees took their breaks, she filled her mug with coffee, gulped a swallow, then swore when the hot liquid burned her tongue.

"Careful," a female voice warned from behind her. "Lawsuits have been fought and won over the scalding effects of hot coffee."

She whipped her head around to find that Deirdre had entered the room. Grimacing, she dropped down onto a chair at the table. "Haven't you heard? You can't fight city hall."

Chuckling, Deirdre took a seat opposite Andi. "You've got a point."

"What are you doing here?" Andi asked in puzzlement. "I thought you were working graveyard this month."

"I am, but I had to finish up an arrest report. A couple of teenagers decided to celebrate their newly earned high school senior status by spray painting the city water tower."

Andi sank back against her chair with a dramatic sigh. "Ah, youth. Those were the days."

"Yeah, then you grow up and find out that life sucks."

Andi drew back to look at Deirdre in surprise. "My, but aren't you the cynical one today."

"Can't argue with the facts. Things are easier when you're young."

Noticing the dark circles under her friend's eyes, Andi attributed her current mood to exhaustion. She leaned forward and gave her hand a comforting pat. "You're just tired. Go home and get some rest. You'll feel differently after you've gotten a good eight hours sleep."

Wearily, Deirdre pushed to her feet. "Yeah, you're probably right." At the door, she stopped and glanced back. "By the way, how are things going with you and Gabe? Are the two of you getting along all right?"

Andi snorted a breath. "Depends on your definition of 'all right.'"

"He's not coming on to you, is he?"

"Wouldn't matter if he was," Andi informed her.

"I'm not interested in Gabe Thunderhawk." She flapped a hand. "Even if I was, he's too young for me."

"Oh, come on. Seven years isn't that big a gap."

"That would depend on which side of the gap you're standing on. Unfortunately, my view is from the far side."

"Just be careful," Deirdre warned. "Gabe can be charming when he wants to be, but he's a user. Trust me. I know. I've got the footprints to prove it." She flapped a hand. "But that's old news. I've got a new guy in my sights."

"Really?" Andi said, unaware that her friend had a new boyfriend. "Who?"

Deirdre shook her head as she walked out. "If I tell you, it might jinx it. And I don't want to take a chance on blowing it with this guy."

Andi frowned as Deirdre turned down the hall, puzzled by her friend's refusal to share her new boyfriend's name. She certainly hadn't been hesitant to share the details of her past relationships, including the one with Gabe. Her frown deepened as she recalled Deirdre's warning about Gabe. Odd, but she couldn't remember her ever mentioning having any ill feelings toward Gabe. In fact, according to Deirdre, he all but hung the moon. So why had she warned Andi to be careful around him?

With a sigh, she pushed away from the table.

Doesn't matter, she told herself as she headed back to the patrol room. She didn't need to be warned away from Gabe Thunderhawk. Unlike Deirdre, who slipped from one bad relationship to another in her almost desperate search for Mr. Right, Andi didn't want or need a man in her life. She'd come to that conclusion her senior year in college. And it wasn't from something she'd learned in the classroom. She'd been taught that particular lesson in a bedroom.

Deirdre unlocked her apartment, then stooped to pick up the morning paper and scanned the headlines as she stepped inside. The door slammed shut behind her and she whirled, her hand going instinctively to the gun holstered at her waist.

"You're late."

Laughing weakly, she dropped her hand from the gun. "Have you ever heard of knocking?"

He lifted a brow. "I can leave, if you want."

Dropping the newspaper, she wound her arms around his neck and smiled coyly up at him as she rubbed her body against his. "No way, buster. I've been thinking about this all night."

"Thinking about what?" he asked as he slipped a hand between her legs. "This?" He cupped her mound and lifted, drawing her to her toes.

"Oh, yes," she moaned as he dug his fingers into her center.

"Damn, you're already wet." Keeping his hand cupped on her mound, he urged her backward.

She closed her eyes and focused her mind on the increasing pressure of his fingers.

The back of her knees hit the edge of the sofa and she fell back, letting her legs sprawl wide. He planted a knee into the V, then ripped open her shirt and filled his hands with her breasts.

She dropped her head back on a moan.

"Tell me what you want," he whispered as he kneaded the soft flesh.

She dragged a bra strap down her shoulder, baring a breast. "Suck me."

She groaned as he opened his mouth over her breast, then clamped her legs against his knee and arched hard against it as he drew her nipple in.

"Touch me," she begged as she stripped off her holster and opened her slacks.

He pushed her hand aside and slid his hand inside her panties.

"Yes," she whispered as he pushed a knuckle along her folds. "Oh, yes!" she cried, wincing as he drove a finger inside.

He slowly pulled it out, then spread the moisture around her opening. "You like it rough, don't you, baby?"

She fought her slacks down her hips and spread her legs wider, offering herself to him.

He stabbed his finger inside. "Nobody can please you the way I can, can they?"

Nearly crazy with need, she dropped her head back against the sofa, willing to agree to almost anything if he'd make her climax. "Nobody."

"Not even that Indian?"

"No. Not even him."

He pulled his hand out and ripped down his zipper, freed his sex.

Taking it in his hand, he waved it back and forth, teasing her with it. "Want this, baby?"

She stared, her eyes glazed with passion, her body on fire. "Yes," she whispered and reached for it.

He drew back. "If you want it, you have to ask really nice."

"Please," she sobbed.

"Where do you want it?" He stroked it along her folds. "Here?"

She filled her hands with her breasts and squeezed her eyes shut. "Yes, there. Please. There."

He pressed his erection against her opening. "Here?"

She arched high, straining. "Yes!" she sobbed. "Oh, please. Give it to me. Now!"

He drove deep and she opened her mouth to cry out her pleasure, but he clamped a hand over her lips, smothering the sound.

"Shh," he soothed. "You don't want your neighbors to hear, do you?"

Her eyes wild and fixed on his, she shook her head.

Smiling, he dragged his hand from her mouth and closed it over her breast. "I didn't think you did." He caught her nipple between finger and thumb, and she closed her eyes again, moaning low in her throat as he pinched them together.

Nobody understood her the way he did, she thought as pain and pleasure lanced her womb.

Nobody.

Andi unlocked the back door of her house and pushed it open, eager to change her clothes and get back outside and to work. If she hustled, she figured she had enough time to scrape the paint off at least half the rear of her house before the sun set. Maybe all of it, if the light held out long enough. She'd originally planned to tackle the job on Saturday, but the chief had thrown a wrench into her plans with his insistence that she and Gabe go to the charity ball.

But she wasn't going to think about that now, she told herself, feeling the irritation rising. If she did, it would put her in a bad mood.

Mentally listing the tools she'd need, she quickly stripped out of her clothes and tugged on a pair of old shorts and a T-shirt. As she retraced her steps to the kitchen, she wrapped a bandana around her head to keep paint chips from matting in her hair, then stopped to check the messages on her answering machine.

"Hi, this is Melissa from Dr. Andrews's office calling to remind you of your dental appointment tomorrow morning at nine. If you're unable to make the appointment, please call our office and reschedule."

She shuddered at the reminder of her annual dental exam, then deleted the message and waited for the next one to play. But no voice came through the speaker. Only the hum of recorded silence, then a *click*. Frowning, she hit the back button and checked the caller ID. *Unknown.* Her frown deepening, she punched the delete button. That was the third hang-up she'd received that week. One a month was rare.

When she'd moved into her house, she'd requested an unlisted telephone number, a precaution that most officers on the force took to protect their privacy, as well as their safety. There were a select few with whom she had entrusted her number. The dispatcher at the station, her dentist, her doctor, a couple of friends, a few distant relatives. So why so many hang-ups? she asked herself.

"Probably an overzealous telemarketer," she told herself and headed out the door.

Once in the backyard, she dragged the ladder

from the patio, propped it against the side of the house and plugged in the electric sander. Armed with a paint scraper to use on the tight spots the sander couldn't reach and a pair of safety goggles, she climbed the ladder and set to work. Paint chips flew around her face and speckled her arms and legs. She slowly made her way down the ladder, moving the sander over the wood. When she reached the bottom, she repositioned the ladder, then set to work again.

Not that she considered this work.

To her, the improvements she made on her home, whether they were made weeding her flower beds or refinishing the old wood flooring inside, were nothing but true pleasure. She'd purchased the house two years prior and had spent every spare moment since remodeling and redecorating it, both inside and out. The bonus she'd discovered was that it was the perfect way to relieve the stress associated with her job.

She was level with her bedroom window when she noticed the scratches along the lower edge of the screen. She quickly switched off the sander and shifted on the ladder in order to examine them more closely. Judging by the depth of the cuts along the aluminum frame, it appeared someone had attempted to pry off the screen. Whoever it was had failed in his mission, since the screen was still securely latched.

Most women would've panicked at the thought of a prowler trying to break into their house and would've run for the nearest phone to call the police. Not Andi. She *was* the police. Her only emotion at the moment was anger, and it was a toss-up as to what made her more mad: the damage done to her screen or the fact that someone had attempted to break into her house.

With her mouth set in an angry line, she climbed down from the ladder and set aside the sander. Sinking to a knee, she examined the ground beneath the window. The mulch spread around the shrubs and flowers in the bed that lined the back wall was over three inches thick and well packed, which negated any chance of finding a clear footprint.

Frustrated, she stood, bracing her hands on her hips as she looked around, trying to figure out how the prowler might have gained entry. The privacy fence that enclosed her backyard on three sides was covered in flowering vines she'd planted during the two years she'd owned the home, which made scaling the fence difficult, if not impossible.

Beyond the fence were her neighbors—the Huckabees at the rear, whom she knew only in passing; Mr. and Mrs. Brown on the right, a dear, elderly couple with whom she enjoyed visiting when she was out working in her yard or on her house; and Richard Givens on the left, a fiftysomething divorcé, who considered himself God's gift to women.

She shuddered in revulsion at the thought of Richard, with his bleached-blond hair, fake-bake tan and thick gold rope chain he wore around his neck, a throwback from the disco era, no doubt. He'd made more passes at her than a professional quarterback and continued to do so even after she'd repeatedly told him she wasn't interested. But the man had an ego the size of Dallas and a hide as thick as a rhinoceros, which obviously made him impervious to her refusals.

Frowning, she peered at the iron gate that opened from the side yard that ran between her house and Richard's, the only other means of gaining entry to her backyard. She kept the gate locked at all times, unless she was outside. But she supposed a person could climb over it, if they wanted to badly enough. Richard was certainly physically capable of scaling the gate, but she couldn't imagine why he would want to get inside her house.

She heard the familiar squeal of tires on the driveway next door and groaned, knowing it was Richard arriving home. A red Corvette braked to a stop in front of his garage. Yesterday he'd been driving a BMW coupe. An unending supply of cars to choose from was one of the many perks he enjoyed as the owner of a used-car lot.

Hoping to escape before he saw her, she grabbed her sander and started up the ladder.

"Hi, Andrea! Working on the house again?"

Stifling another groan, she stopped and forced a polite smile. "Yeah. I'm trying to get the rear wall scraped before it gets too dark to see."

He wagged a stern finger. "All work and no play makes Andrea a dull girl." Grinning, he motioned for her to join him. "Come on over and I'll mix us up a batch of martinis."

"Sorry, but I'll have to take a rain check." She hefted the sander for him to see. "Duty calls."

"Ah, come on," he wheedled. "Surely you've got time for one of my famous dry martinis."

She set her jaw to keep from screaming her frustration. "No, Richard, I really don't."

His smile slipped a bit at her refusal, then he shrugged and turned away. "Your loss."

Staring, she choked a laugh. *My* loss? Shaking her head, she started up the ladder again. The guy was crazy. Certifiably insane. She stopped, her smile fading as she remembered the attempted break-in. No, she told herself, and resumed her climbing. Richard was a nuisance, but he wasn't a criminal.

Or at least she didn't think he was.

Shaking off the thought, she flipped on the sander. At the same moment, her cell phone rang. Muttering a curse, she shut off the machine and tugged the phone from the clip at her waist. "Mat-thews," she snapped into the receiver.

"We've got a stabbing out on Maynor Road. Pete's Place."

She frowned, surprised to hear Gabe's voice and not that of the dispatcher on duty. "Why are you calling me and not Joe?"

"Because I'm at the station and Joe has his hands full."

She glanced at her wristwatch, gauging the time. "I'll meet you there in fifteen minutes."

"It'll be faster if I swing by and pick you up."

"No, I—" Before she could tell him she preferred to drive herself, there was a click and then the dial tone.

Furious that he'd hung up on her, she shoved the phone back onto its clip at her waist and stomped her way down the ladder.

She showered and changed clothes in record time and was locking her front door when Gabe pulled up in front of her house.

With her mouth set in a hard line, she climbed into the passenger seat and slammed the door. "I don't need a chauffeur," she informed him tersely, "and if you hadn't hung up on me, I could've told you that on the phone."

He spared her a glance. "Are you this bitchy with everybody or do you reserve all your anger for me?"

Jutting her chin, she faced the windshield. "You rub me the wrong way."

He put the truck in gear. "That's odd. I don't recall laying a hand on you."

Before she could think of a smart comeback, he stomped the accelerator and the truck shot forward, thrusting Andi back against the seat. She wanted to demand that he slow down, but remembered the last time that she'd commented on his driving he'd considered it a dare, and decided not to push her luck.

"What's the situation at Pete's Place?" she asked, hoping if she distracted him, he'd slow down on his own.

"Stabbing. Jarrod, the new rookie, responded to the call."

"Something's always happening at Pete's Place. Ten to one it's over a woman."

"As much as I'd like to accept your bet, it would be like taking candy from a baby."

She gave him a droll look. "I take it you don't think it started over a woman."

He took a turn on two wheels, then shook his head. "No. Fights over women usually take place nearer to closing time, when folks start to pair off."

She lifted a brow. "Is that the voice of experience speaking?"

"No. Common sense."

"Okay, if not a woman, then what do you think started it?"

He made a sharp turn into the parking lot of Pete's and braked to a rock-spitting stop behind the patrol car already at the scene. "Most of the men who hang out at Pete's are construction workers. My guess is that it's a disagreement they brought with them from the job."

She reached for the door handle. "Well, let's see which one of us is right."

It appeared that the entire bar had emptied into the parking lot to watch the fight. Customers and employees alike formed a human wall that Gabe and Andi had to shoulder their way through before finding their victim. He sat on the ground beside a truck, his back propped against its rear tire, holding a blood-soaked cloth against his left arm. More blood was spattered on his shirt and jeans. Jarrod, the rookie cop, was standing off to the side, shooting the breeze with the ambulance driver.

Setting her jaw, Andi stalked toward him. "What the hell do you think you're doing?"

The rookie jerked to attention. "Nothing, sir— I—I mean, ma'am."

"Well, that's obvious," she snapped, then pointed a stiff finger at the victim. "Do you realize that man might very well be bleeding to death while you're over here flapping your jaws?"

"Uh, yes, ma'am. I tried to get him to let the

paramedics load him up in the ambulance, but he won't let anybody near him."

Making a mental note to discuss later with the rookie his inability to control a scene, she turned for the victim, but found Gabe had beat her there. Judging by the conversation between the two, it appeared they knew each other.

"Hey, Dal," she heard Gabe say. "How bad is it, buddy?"

"Pretty bad," Dal said, then gulped and began to unwind the crude bandage he held on his arm. "He cut me deep."

Andi winced as Dal exposed the gaping wound.

"It's deep all right," Gabe confirmed. "Looks like he sliced you clear to the bone. We need to get you to a hospital."

Dal drew back against the tire and shook his head. "No. Ain't got the money to ride in no ambulance. My brother Bill'll be gettin' off work soon. He'll take me."

"What time does Bill get off?"

"Works the four-to-eleven shift over at a convenience store in San Antonio."

His expression grim, Gabe pushed his hands against his thighs. "I can't let you sit here and bleed to death, while you wait on your brother."

Dal kept his eyes fixed on Gabe, as Gabe stood. "I ain't goin' in no ambulance. I told you, I ain't got the money to pay."

"You're not going in the ambulance," Gabe informed him. "You're going with me."

Shocked, Andi watched as Gabe helped Dal to his feet. When he began guiding the man to his truck, she quickly fell in behind them.

"Who did this to you?" she heard Gabe asked Dal.

"Whitey. A guy on my crew. Had to fire him today. Can't have a man on the payroll who thinks he can come and go whenever he pleases."

Andi stifled a groan. Gabe didn't so much as glance her way, but she heard his "I told you so" as clearly as if he'd shouted it at the top of his lungs.

Chapter 3

Andi didn't question Gabe's decision to personally escort Dal to the hospital. And she didn't question him when he gave his own mailing address to the nurse on duty and told her to send him Dal's bill. But by the time they were back in his truck and headed for her house, the questions were burning holes in her tongue.

"Taking a victim to the hospital isn't part of the job," she said, seeking a noncombative opening.

"I know."

"So why did you do it?"

He stopped at a stop sign, waited for a car to cross the intersection, then drove on. "You heard him. He couldn't afford an ambulance ride."

"That's not your fault, nor your responsibility."

"No," he agreed. "But I wasn't about to let him sit there and bleed to death while he waited for his brother. I doubt you would've, either."

"No," she agreed, "but I sure as heck wouldn't have offered to pay for his medical care."

"He'll make good the debt."

She gave him a doubtful look. "Come on, Gabe. If he couldn't afford to ride in an ambulance, do you really think he can come up with the money to pay a hospital bill?"

"Dal might not have the cash on hand, but he's an honest man and a damn good framer. I've been wanting to build a storage shed behind the cabin." He lifted a shoulder. "He can work off the loan."

She stared, unable to associate this kind gesture with the Gabe Thunderhawk she knew. Or, rather, the Gabe Thunderhawk she *thought* she knew. His rep around the station was that of a tough cop, one who didn't have to ask a perp twice for his cooperation. Most of them took one look at him and fell to the pavement, offering their wrists for the cuffs.

"Do you have a boyfriend?"

She blinked, startled by the unexpected question, then frowned. "Not that it's any of your business, but no. Why?"

He glanced at the rearview mirror. "Someone's following us. Just wanted to make sure it wasn't your boyfriend, before I tried to lose him."

She whipped her head around to look out the rear window but couldn't see anything but the glare of headlights from the car behind. "Are you sure he's following us? He could be just headed in the same direction."

"He's been on our tail ever since we left the hospital. Hold on," he warned. "We're going to see how badly he wants us."

She grabbed for the chicken bar as he spun the wheel to the right and took a corner on two wheels. When the truck leveled out to all four tires, he glanced at the rearview mirror again. "Must not want us too badly."

He sped up and took the next left, doubling back to the street they'd originally been traveling on. He stopped at the intersection and looked both ways. "Lost him. He must've realized we'd made him." He turned right and raced down the street, but whoever had been tailing them had disappeared from sight.

"Do you have any enemies?" he asked.

She frowned, remembering the bent screen she'd discovered at her house earlier that evening. "None that I'm aware of." She glanced his way. "But why assume he was after me? He could've been following you. We're in your truck, after all."

"Maybe. Cops have more enemies than friends. Detectives even more. Has anyone you've put behind bars been released lately?"

She searched her mind and could come up with only one name. "Dudley Harris was released three months ago."

"The wife beater?"

She flattened her lips as she recalled the details of the case. "One and the same. Served six months of a two-year sentence. Got out on good behavior."

"Do you know where he lives?"

"I know where he *used* to live. His wife sold their house and moved away not long after he went to prison."

"Smart lady."

"Not always. She let him use her for a punching bag for years before we finally persuaded her to press charges." She shook her head sadly. "She was scared to death of him. Made excuses for him all the time. Claimed it was her fault he knocked her around."

"That's not unusual in cases of abuse. Once the cops arrive, the wife usually changes her story and ends up taking the blame for what happened."

"Yeah," she agreed bitterly. "Because she knows if she doesn't, she'll get a worse beating after the cops leave."

"Harris probably holds you responsible for him losing his wife and home. Could be he's looking to even the score." He pulled up in front of her house and shoved the gearshift into Park. "I'll go inside and take a look around."

She reached for the door handle. "If you think I'm afraid to go into my own house alone, you're wrong. Dudley Harris doesn't scare me."

She climbed down, but when she rounded the front of the truck, she found Gabe waiting for her at the end of the sidewalk. "I don't need your protection," she informed him. "I can take care of myself."

He opened his hands. "Who said anything about protecting you? My mother would skin my hide if she knew I'd dumped a lady on the side of the street without properly seeing her to her door."

Scowling, she pushed past him. "Tell her you did. I'll back up your story if she questions your honesty."

He fell into step behind her. "I'd never lie to my mother."

She shot him a frown over her shoulder.

He lifted his hands. "Even if I tried, she'd see right through the lie. I swear, the woman is a living and breathing lie detector machine. Growing up, she knew I was fibbing before I ever spun the yarn."

In spite of her frustration with him, Andi had to bite back a smile as she dug in her shoulder bag for her key, imagining Gabe as a young boy. "I'll bet you were a handful."

"No more so than my brothers."

She inserted the key in the lock, then glanced his way. "Brothers? As in plural?"

"Yeah. Five, to be exact."

Her eyes opened wide. *"Five?"* At his nod, she released a long breath. "Wow. I can't imagine what it would be like to grow up with that many kids in one house."

"How many brothers and sisters do you have?"

"None. I'm an only child." She turned the key and pushed open the door. When he would have followed her in, she shifted to block his way. "You've seen me to my door. Your mother will be proud."

"Did I mention that she expected me to go inside and check all the windows and doors, and look under the bed?"

She folded her arms across her chest. "Nice try, but if there are any bogeymen waiting for me, I'll take care of them myself."

He leaned to peer around her. "Is that your cat?"

She whipped her head around. "I don't have a—"

Gabe used the distraction to slip by her.

Realizing she'd been duped, she flattened her lips in a scowl. "That trick is as old as I am."

He started down the hall toward the kitchen. "You fell for it, didn't you?"

She shut the door and marched after him. "This is ridiculous. I don't need you to search my house."

He flipped on the back porch light, then lifted the drape over the window above the sink to peer outside. "You've got a message on your answering machine. You might want to check it."

Andi whipped her gaze to the telephone and was surprised to see that the message light was, in fact, blinking. Frowning, she hit the play button. Ten seconds of recorded silence was followed by a click.

He glanced her way. "Do you get a lot of hang-ups?"

Avoiding his gaze, she punched Delete. "No more than the next person."

He dropped the drape and turned. "Has the number increased lately?"

"What is this?" she asked impatiently. "An interrogation?"

"Yeah. So do I need to get out the bright lights or are you going to answer my question?"

She sagged her shoulders in defeat. "Okay, so maybe I've received a few more than usual, but that doesn't mean someone is gunning for me."

He headed for the hallway. Andi charged after him. "Where do you think you're going now?"

"To your bedroom."

She stood in tight-lipped silence, watching as he peered under her bed, then opened her closet door. He shoved the hanging clothes to one side and looked in. When he was satisfied that no one was hiding there, he dragged the hangers back into place and started to close the door. He stopped, then reached in and drew something out.

Andi's cheeks flamed in embarrassment when she saw that he was holding her black teddy.

He held it up by a crooked finger. "Would you mind modeling this for me?"

She snatched it from his hand, then pointed to the door. "Out."

He shrugged. "Can't blame a man for trying."

"Out," she repeated.

Smiling, he stuffed his hands into his pockets and headed for the hallway. Andi followed to make sure that he left. At the front door, she stopped, watching as he continued down the walk toward his truck.

"If you get scared," he called over his shoulder, "you know where I live."

She rolled her eyes. "I wouldn't hold my breath if I were you."

He climbed inside his truck, then rolled down the window and shot her a wink. "Wear that little black thing and I might even let you sleep in my bed."

Andi stood before Leo's recliner, eyeing her regular partner critically. "How much weight have you lost?"

"I don't know. Thirty pounds or so."

"And your doctor is okay with that?"

Scowling, he turned his gaze to the television screen and punched the remote, changing the channel. "You're as bad as Myrna. Bunch of hens clucking around me all the time. Can't even take a leak without somebody tagging along to watch."

Accustomed to Leo's grouchiness, Andi bit back a smile. "Where is Myrna, anyway?"

"Went to the movies with her girlfriends. Said she'd had about all the togetherness she could stand. I say good riddance. I've had about all I can take of her, too."

Laughing, Andi dropped a kiss on his bald head. "If I didn't know you were nuts about each other, I'd worry."

"The old bag's been hanging around for thirty-seven years. Can't see dumping her now."

"Good thing. You'd never find another woman as good as Myrna."

"I guess she's all right."

Which in Leo-talk meant he was crazy about her. Chuckling, Andi dragged over a stool to sit at his feet. "So when are you scheduled to see the doctor again?"

He gave her a bored look. "Why don't you quit beating around the bush and tell me what's on your mind? I know damn good and well you didn't come over to discuss my health."

She wanted to deny that anything was troubling her, but she knew she couldn't fool Leo. Sometimes it seemed he knew her better than she knew herself. "It's Gabe," she admitted reluctantly.

"If he's not carrying his share of the workload, just give me the word and I'll come up to the station and whup his ass."

Chuckling, she closed her hand over Leo's on the armrest and gave it a squeeze. "And you would, too."

"Damn straight."

Growing serious, she drew her hand back to her lap. "It's not his work ethic. I can't fault him there."

"Then what's the problem?"

Unsure how to voice her concerns, she stood and began to pace. "Chief Prater is making us go to the charity ball at the country club Saturday night. He thinks we can pick up a lead there on the Lost Fortune case."

"Free food and liquor? Where's the complaint?"

"Gabe keeps referring to it as a date."

"Ahhh," he said, nodding knowingly. "So that's the problem."

"And what's that supposed to mean?"

"You're a woman, he's a man." He opened his hands. "The juices were bound to start flowing sooner or later."

She flattened her lips. "You and I have been partners for nine years and I've never even *once* thought about having sex with you."

"And you're thinking about having sex with Gabe."

She stiffened, realizing what she'd said. She considered telling Leo that his heart attack must have affected his hearing, because that wasn't what she'd said, at all.

Instead, she sank to the stool and dropped her forehead to her hands. "I don't know what I'm thinking," she said miserably. "One minute I want to claw his eyes out and the next I'm mentally undressing him."

"Sounds like love to me."

She jerked her head up to glare. "I am *not* in love with him."

"In lust, then."

She gave him a droll look. "Leo, I'm thirty-six. Lust is reserved for teenagers and twentysomethings."

"Hell, I'm sixty-two and I still get a kick out of chasing Myrna around the bedroom."

Wincing, she held up a hand. "Please. I can do without that visual."

"You think sex is only for kids? Hell, the older a person gets the better *it* gets."

"Leo!" she cried.

He raised his hands. "All right. All right. I won't say any more." He lifted a brow. "But I feel I should warn you. Pipes can rust from lack of use."

She leaped to her feet, her cheeks burning. "That's it," she said, and headed for the door. "I'm getting out of here."

Laughing, he called after her, "Next time you come over, bring Gabe with you. I want to hear the details of y'all's *date*."

Though it irritated Andi every time she thought about Leo referring to her assignment with Gabe at the country club as a date, by Saturday night even *she* had to admit she felt as if she was preparing for one.

She'd spent over two hours showering, styling her hair and applying her makeup, then burned another hour agonizing over what to wear. The dress she'd finally settled on was a simple black sheath, with a hemline that struck her legs at midcalf. A cowl collar at the neckline dipped in front to reveal a hint of cleavage.

With her gaze fixed critically on her reflection in the mirror, she adjusted the cowl collar higher over her breasts, then twisted around to peer at the back, where the collar plunged to an inch below her waist, exposing a daring amount of bare skin.

"I did not choose this dress to impress Gabe Thunderhawk," she said for the zillionth time since putting it on.

Unfortunately her conscience still refused to buy the story.

Sagging her shoulders in defeat, she turned to face the mirror again. Okay, so maybe she had chosen it with him in mind. But it was his fault that she was thinking of him at all! He was the one who kept trying to put an intimate spin on what should be a professional relationship.

Frowning, she glanced at her closet, remembering him standing in front of it with her black teddy dangling from the tip of his index finger. And the nerve of the guy, offering to share his bed with her if she'd wear it. Did he ever think about anything other than sex?

Convinced that he didn't, she dropped a tube of lipstick into her evening bag and checked her reflection in the mirror one last time. Leaning close to the mirror, she touched a finger beneath her lower lash to smooth away a smudge of mascara. The makeup was overkill in her estimation, but necessary for a black-tie event at the country club. And the upswept hairstyle had taken forever to arrange, but again a requirement if one wanted to mix and mingle with the rich and famous and not stick out like a sore thumb.

The doorbell sounded, signaling Gabe's arrival. She glanced at her watch and frowned, noting that, as usual, he was late. She quickly slipped her feet into the three-inch black slings she'd laid out, knowing full well she'd regret the choice before the night was over, and hurried to the front of the house. She took a moment to draw in a calming breath, then opened the door. It lodged in her throat at her first glimpse of him.

She'd half expected him to defy the chief's order to wear a tux, but he was wearing one...or parts of one. He had on the slacks—thank God—and he held the jacket draped over his shoulder by a crooked finger. It was the shirt that was the problem. Technically she supposed he was wearing it. But he hadn't bothered to tuck in the tails or button it up, which left a large portion of his chest exposed.

Slowly she lifted her gaze to his. "Have you lost your mind?" she asked in disbelief, then shot a frantic glance behind him to see if anyone was looking. "What will my neighbors think?"

"That you have a hot date?"

Flattening her lips, she dragged him inside and quickly closed the door behind him. "This isn't a date."

"So you keep saying." He tossed the jacket over the back of a chair. "I told the guy at the rental place that I hated bow ties. He suggested this collarless shirt. Said it was formal enough, as long as I wore these." He opened his hand, to reveal a tangle of black onyx studs. "Unfortunately, he failed to mention how to attach them."

She huffed a breath and snatched one from his palm. "If you'd asked, I'm sure he would've been more than happy to show you."

"Uh-uh," he said, shaking his head. "No way was I letting that guy anywhere near my body."

He opened his arms in invitation. "But you, on the other hand, have my permission to touch me anywhere you want."

She burned him with a look before stabbing the post through the slot beside the top-most button.

"Hey!" he cried, flinching as the post dug into his skin. "I said you could touch, not maim."

"Sorry," she muttered, though she didn't feel so much as a morsel of regret.

As she tugged the black disk through the button hole, she gathered her irritation with him around her like a shield, using it to protect her from the intimacy of the act she performed.

But after attaching only two studs, she discovered her irritation was no match for his maleness. Not when her knuckles brushed his bare skin each time she inserted a post. And not when, with each breath she drew, she inhaled an intoxicating blend of sandalwood and pure male.

She heard a low hum of approval and glanced up to find his gaze fixed on her chest. Realizing that, with her arms lifted, her dress gaped to reveal an embarrassing amount of her breasts, she quickly dropped her arms and took a step back.

"Do you want my help or not?"

He rolled his lips inward to hide a smile. "You know I do."

"Then close your eyes. And no peeking," she warned.

She waited until he'd followed her instructions, then set to work again.

After fitting the last stud into place, she breathed a sigh of relief. "Done."

He opened his eyes and smiled. "Thanks." He unfastened the hook at the waist of his slacks and turned his back to her. "How long do you think we'll have to stay at this shindig?"

She stared, unable to believe that he had unfastened his slacks in front of her. She started to look away, but the scrape of his zipper seemed to freeze her gaze, and she continued to stare, mesmerized, as he stuffed his shirttail into the waistband of his slacks. It was such a simple act, yet so utterly... *male.*

"I—I don't know," she stammered.

He tugged up the zipper, then faced her again and gave her a quick look up and down. "That's a hot little number you're wearing. Let's see the back."

Before she could dodge him, he'd clamped his hands on her shoulders and was angling her around.

"No," he corrected, his voice dropping an octave. "It's downright sinful."

She could feel the heat of his gaze sliding from the nape of her neck to her waist and closed her eyes, suddenly dizzy.

He smoothed his hands down her arms and dipped his face to her ear as he linked his fingers with hers. She stifled a shiver, unable to remember the last time a man had touched her in this way. The sensual abrade of flesh skimming over flesh. The heat of a man's body pressed close to hers. The moist warmth of his breath caressing her ear. It would be so easy to let her head loll back against his shoulder, offer her neck to his mouth, his lips. To feel again the hot rush of desire as it spread through her body.

But that would be giving in to her more basic needs, exposing a weakness that could be taken advantage of. She'd learned over the years that the only way to resist lust was to avoid it all together.

Knowing that, she stepped from his embrace and away from temptation.

"Good job," she said as she reached for her evening bag. Pasting on a smile, she turned and gave his cheek a proud pat. "If you can keep up that act, no one at the country club will ever suspect that we're there to spy on them."

From the porte cochere where costumed valets waited to park the guests' cars, to the country club's main dining room where champagne flowed from a multispouted fountain into giant silver bowls placed around its base, it was obvious that whoever was in charge of organizing the party had spared no expense.

Arabian Nights was the theme for the evening,

and the huge sheets of boldly striped fabric draped from the ceiling to the corners of the room created the illusion of the interior of a sheik's tent. Waitresses dressed as Arabian princesses and waiters decked out as sultans moved through the crowd, offering guests drinks and hors d'oeuvres from ornate silver trays. The French doors that separated the dining room from the patio were thrown open, allowing peeks of a star-studded sky and giving the guests the freedom to move from one area to the other.

All things considered, Gabe figured this had to rank as the cushiest assignment of his entire career as a policeman. All the food and drink he could consume, and a gorgeous woman at his side? What else could a man ask for?

Frowning, he stole a glance at Andi. A woman without ice in her veins.

What was with her, anyway? he asked himself in frustration. Back at her house, he'd actually thought that he'd finally made some progress with her. When he'd held her in his arms, he would've sworn he'd sensed a response in her, a softening. Then...*boom!* She'd shut him down.

An act, she'd called it, his frown deepening as he recalled her congratulating him on a job well done. Hell, that was no act! At least, it hadn't been for him.

But maybe it had been for her, he realized slowly.

He'd worked undercover enough to know it was easy enough for a person to successfully adopt a different persona. He'd once assumed the role of a biker in order to infiltrate a motorcycle gang thought to be running drugs. He'd played the part so well that when the bust had taken place, one of the guys on the force had slapped cuffs on him before Gabe could convince him he was one of the good guys.

But if that was the case, the question now was, which one was the act? Which of the personas he'd interacted with that evening was the real Andrea Matthews, and which was a role she was playing? The hot little vixen who'd shivered in his arms? Or the cool by-the-book detective who had commended him on a job well done?

To hell with it, he thought irritably. He wasn't in the mood for games. Either the woman was interested or she wasn't. It was no skin off his back either way.

Wishing the evening would hurry up and end, he took Andi by the elbow. "I need some air."

"Did you see Ryan Fortune?" she whispered to him as he ushered her out the French doors. "He was over by the chocolate fountain talking to Melissa Wilkes. They seemed awfully friendly. Do you think something could be going on between them?"

Gabe braced his hips against the limestone balustrade surrounding the patio. "I don't know," he replied sourly, then tipped his head in the direction of the dining room. "But it appears his wife shares your concern. She's had her eye on him all evening and looks none too happy that Melissa's with him."

She shifted to stand beside him, in order to get a better view of the dining room's interior. "I see what you mean," she said, then looked up at him with a frown. "Do you remember the day we took Lily and Ryan to the M.E.'s office to identify the floater? She had that same look on her face then. Tight-lipped. Wary. As if she didn't quite trust him."

"Yeah, I remember." He lifted a shoulder. "Maybe he's having a midlife crisis. An affair is one of the symptoms. Has he purchased a Harley recently?"

She choked a laugh. "Ryan on a Harley?" She shook her head. "He's not the type. I can't imagine him cheating on his wife."

He looked at her in disbelief. "What is it with you? Ever since we were assigned this case, you've wanted to pin the murder on Ryan. Why the sudden change of heart?"

She lifted her chin defensively. "Murder and adultery are two entirely different matters. Just because a person is capable of one doesn't mean he could commit the other." She flapped a hand. "Besides, Ryan adores Lily. Everybody knows that. He'd never cheat on her."

"I wouldn't be so sure. When a man starts questioning his virility, he'll do almost anything to prove he's still macho. And age isn't always the catalyst," he added. "Men in their thirties and forties can suffer the same doubts. A tumble in bed with a hot, young babe is like a shot of adrenaline for their egos. A way for them to prove that they've still got it."

He watched the blood slowly drain from her face. "What?" he asked, in confusion.

She twisted around to face the gardens and shook her head. "Nothing."

Frowning, he studied her profile, wondering what he'd said that would warrant that kind of reaction. Hell, a person would think he'd slapped her! But since they'd been discussing the possibility of Ryan Fortune having an affair, he had to believe that was what had stripped the color from her face and put that stricken look in her eyes. If so...why?

Though the urge to push for answers was strong, he suppressed it, knowing this wasn't the time or place. They were here to do a job. Reminded of that, he glanced around the patio and was surprised to see that a few couples appeared to have noticed Andi's reaction and were eyeing her strangely. Knowing the less attention they drew to themselves, the better, he took her hand. "Let's take a walk."

When she resisted, he tightened his grip and said in a low voice, "Come on. People are watching."

She glanced up, saw that what he'd claimed was true, then ducked her head in embarrassment and allowed him to guide her to the steps that led down to a garden.

Luminaries lined the flagstone path that wound through the garden, offering a quiet and shadowed refuge for guests anxious to escape the noise and press of the party. Gabe kept his pace slow, relaxed, giving Andi time to regain her composure before he broached the subject of Ryan Fortune again.

"You know," he said thoughtfully, "Lily's distrust might have nothing to do with another woman and everything to do with the murder."

"We interviewed Lily," she reminded him. "The same as we did every other Fortune. She claimed she didn't know the identity of our floater."

"Maybe she was telling the truth. But that doesn't mean she doesn't know something…like who committed the murder."

She jerked to a stop, drawing Gabe to a stop, as well, her eyes wide in disbelief. "And you accused *me* of having a change of heart? You've done nothing but defend Ryan since day one, and now you think he's the murderer?"

"I wouldn't go that far. I'm just considering all the possibilities. It's obvious that Ryan's wife is worried about something. If not another woman, then it's possible she's concerned about her husband going to prison."

She frowned a moment, considering. "Ryan's a pillar of the community. Wealthy beyond imagination. The one thing that keeps me from believing he is our murderer, is *why?* What reason would he have to kill anyone?"

"You know as well as I do that murderers come in all flavors. As to his reason, who knows? Maybe he was having a bad hair day."

She rolled her eyes. "I'd laugh if I didn't know people were killed for lesser reasons."

"Yeah, it's—" Gabe tensed, cocking his head to listen, sure that he'd heard a noise. He quickly grabbed Andi's hand and tugged her from the path and into the darker shadows beneath the trees.

She tried to pull away. "Get your hands off—"

He clamped a hand over her mouth. "Someone's coming," he whispered.

She immediately stilled.

The sound of footsteps on the stone path grew nearer. Gabe closed his eyes, mentally separating the *click-slap* of a woman's high heels, and the heavier tread of a man's shoes.

"Are you jealous?"

The question was posed by a female, and delivered in a low, sultry purr.

"Of that old man?" a male voice replied, then

snorted a breath. "He probably couldn't even get it up."

The footsteps stopped almost opposite the shadows that concealed Gabe and Andi, and Gabe narrowed his eyes against the darkness, trying to identify the two. The man and woman were facing each other now, their arms looped around each other's waist in a loose embrace. The woman he recognized immediately as Melissa Wilkes, who had been flirting with Ryan Fortune only moments before. The man had his back to him, and Gabe could only guess that he was Jason Wilkes, Melissa's husband.

"Sex isn't everything," Melissa said. "It's the size of a man's bank account that counts, and Ryan Fortune's is plenty big enough for me."

"Liar. You love sex." Chuckling, he moved closer and nuzzled her neck. "Good thing I can satisfy both your sexual needs *and* your greed. Otherwise you might leave me for Ryan."

She gave him a coy look from beneath thick eyelashes. "Honey, no offense. You may be good in bed, but I've seen your checkbook balance and that's chump change compared to Ryan Fortune's wealth."

He hooked a finger beneath her chin and tipped her face up to his. "Stick with me, baby. Before long, I'll have control of Fortune TX, Ltd., and all that money will be ours."

She rubbed against him like a cat. "Mmm. I just love it when you talk dirty." With her gaze on his, she brought his finger to her lips, sucked it in, then slowly pulled it out, flicking her tongue over its tip.

With a groan, Jason crushed his mouth to hers. A lot of moaning and heavy breathing followed, and when Jason finally withdrew, it was with obvious reluctance.

"Later," he promised, his voice husky. "Right now we need to get back to the party. I want to be standing at Ryan's side when he presents our hosts the check from Fortune TX, Ltd."

The couple's footsteps had barely faded when Andi whirled to face Gabe.

"That slut!" she whispered angrily. "Did you hear what she said about Ryan? And to her own husband, no less! She's nothing but a money-hungry bitch."

Gabe dragged a shaky hand down his face, still feeling the effects of having watched Melissa's mouth on her husband's finger. "She definitely knows how to work a man."

Andi stared at him in amazement. "Please tell me you didn't actually fall for that little sex-kitten act?"

"You've got to admit, the woman's got some moves and the body to back them up."

"She's a tease! You heard her. The only thing she's interested in is the size of a man's checkbook.

It's obvious she's using Ryan to make Jason jealous. She's using Ryan's wealth to taunt him into climbing the corporate ladder faster."

"Now wait a minute," Gabe said. "You're making it sound like Jason is the injured party here. Melissa may have her faults, but Wilkes is no saint."

"I can't believe you'd defend her!"

"I'm not defending anybody. I'm merely pointing out the facts. You heard Jason claim that he was going to control Fortune TX, Ltd. Anyone who thinks he can take over the Fortune empire either has an overinflated ego or he's a damn fool. The Fortunes built that company, and you can bet your next paycheck Ryan's not going to stand by and let some junior executive waltz in and take all that away from them."

She folded her arms across her chest and huffed a breath. "If the Fortunes lose control of their empire, the decision won't be made in a boardroom. It'll be in a *bed*room."

"I take it you're referring to Melissa and Ryan."

She opened her hands. "Who else? You fell for her sex-kitten act. What's going to stop Ryan from doing the same?"

The words were barely out of her mouth before she was clamping her lips together and whirling away.

Gabe started after her. "Where are you going?" he asked in frustration.

"To warn Ryan."

He grabbed her arm and jerked her around. "You can't go barreling in there and warn him about Melissa. That's the same as accusing him of having an affair."

Furious, she tugged at her arm. "I'm not accusing him of anything. I only want to warn him."

"Of what? That one of his employees' wives is envious of all his money? Hell, probably half the women in this town would like to get their hands on Ryan Fortune and his bank accounts."

He gave her a shake. "Think about it, Andi. What we overheard could have been nothing more than a woman's wet dream. A carrot she dangles in front of her husband to keep him in line, to give him the kick in the butt she thinks he needs to make him work a little harder for those promotions."

She glared at him a moment longer, then sagged her shoulders in defeat. "Okay," she said grudgingly. "I won't say anything." She set her jaw. "But I'm keeping an eye on her. And if I catch her cuddling up to Ryan again, I'm telling him she's after his money."

Gabe held up his hands. "Fine. Do whatever you feel you have to do. I have only one request. Make damn sure I'm nowhere in the vicinity when you choose to have your heart-to-heart with Ryan."

"Coward," she grumbled. "You'd think you'd—"

While Andi continued to berate him, Gabe tuned

her out and peered beyond her, sure that he heard another sound. Through the shrubs and trees that lined the curving pathway, he caught a flash of movement and knew that someone was headed their way. With no time for explanations, he grabbed Andi and slammed his mouth against hers.

She fought him like a cat, pushing at his chest and squirming within his arms. To keep her from breaking free, he cupped a hand behind her head to hold her mouth to his and vised his arm tighter around her back.

From the corner of his eye, he saw a couple pass by and could tell by their amused expressions that he had succeeded in fooling them into believing that he and Andi had slipped out into the garden for a lover's tryst. He listened to the sound of their footsteps until they grew too faint to hear and knew it was safe to release Andi.

But he didn't let her go.

At some point during the nerve-burning moments while he'd waited for the couple to pass, she'd quit fighting him. Her back was now arched beneath the weight of his arm, a soft bow of need that thrust her breasts against his chest. And her mouth was no longer hard beneath his, but soft and pliant, even hot, as she moved her lips in rhythm with his.

The gentlemanly thing to do would be to end the kiss, explain why he'd chosen to silence her in that manner and pretend he hadn't noticed her re-

sponse. But he'd be a fool to release her now. He'd
suspected that she'd responded to him earlier that
evening while still at her house. Now was as good
a time as any to find out if her response was nothing but an act.

Tightening his arm around her, he drew her up
higher on his chest and parted her lips. The moment
their tongues tangled, an electric shock ripped
through his system, turning him rock hard. Groan-
ing, he shifted, braced his legs wide, and pressed
his erection against her abdomen.

Her response was a low moan of need that vibrated against his mouth and carried to every ex-
tremity. Aroused by the sound, he needed a moment
to realize that she was no longer clinging to him but
was pushing him away.

He dropped his arms and opened his eyes to
find her standing opposite him, her eyes glazed
with passion, her chest heaving. A tendril had es-
caped her upswept hairstyle and draped one flushed
cheek. He reached to brush it aside.

"Andi, I—"

She slapped his hand away. "Don't touch me."

Shocked by her anger, for a moment he could
only stare. By the time he found his voice, she was
twenty feet down the path and all but running.

Gabe pulled up in front of Andi's house and
parked. She hadn't said a word throughout the drive

home, but that was fine with him. He wasn't really interested in listening to anything she had to say... but he had plenty he intended to say to her.

"I've about had all your—"

Before he could say more, she was out of the truck and slamming the door behind her.

He watched her stalk past the front of his truck's hood, then swore and jumped down. "Andi, wait!" he shouted, as he followed her.

She walked faster.

"Andi!" he said furiously, catching her by the arm and spinning her around. "What the hell's wrong with you?"

"I'll tell you what's wrong," she replied, her anger spiking to match his. "I don't appreciate being attacked by my partner."

He caught both her arms and gave her a shake. "Don't you try pulling that sexual harassment line with me. The only thing I'm guilty of is doing my job. While you were busy ranting and raving about Melissa's plot to steal Ryan's money, I saw a couple coming down the path."

"So you kissed me?" she asked incredulously.

"It was the fastest way I could think to shut you up."

She snatched her arms from his grasp and wrapped them around her middle. "A simple *hush* would've sufficed."

"You've gotta be kidding! You were so riled

up over the idea that Melissa was using Ryan, I would've had to coldcock you to get your attention."

"Well, the next time you want my attention," she returned tersely, "you have my permission to hit me. I'd rather suffer a bruise than another one of your kisses."

"Liar."

Her eyes shot wide. "What?"

"You're a liar. You were enjoying that kiss as much as I was."

"I was not!"

He could almost see the smoke coming from her ears. But that didn't stop him. She'd wounded his male pride by insisting that she hadn't enjoyed the kiss, and he intended to get in a few hits of his own to even the score.

Rocking back on his heels, he hitched his hands on his hips. "Oh, really? Then what was with all the tongue thrusts and grinding of hips?"

He watched the color drain from her face and knew he'd hit his mark. He decided to dig the knife a little deeper. "When a woman responds like that, it kinda makes a guy wonder how long it's been since she's had sex."

Her mouth dropped open, then closed with a click of teeth so loud it sounded like a gunshot in the night.

"This is ridiculous," she said and whirled for

the house. "I refuse to discuss this with you any longer."

"Go ahead and run," he shouted after her. "Doesn't change a thing. You're still a liar. And a tease!" he added, raising his voice to make sure she heard him.

Chapter 4

It was Sunday and an absolutely gorgeous day outside, the kind of day Andi would normally spend working on her house or in her garden. But the day was already half-gone and she stood in front of her breakfast room window wearing the oversized T-shirt she'd slept in, staring out at nothing.

Her eyes burned from lack of sleep, and fingers of pain shot through her skull with each beat of her pulse, making her head throb even worse. She had a blister on her foot, thanks to the three-inch heels she'd worn the night before, and she was sure she felt the beginnings of a zit on the side of her nose, a malady she hadn't experienced since the high school prom.

And it was *all* Gabe's fault.

He'd called her a liar. Standing in front of her own home and in full view of her neighbors, he'd called her a liar.

And a tease.

That was the worst. Liar she could deal with. After all, it was the truth. She *had* lied to him. But what woman would willingly admit that she'd responded to a man? Especially when that man was throwing the response in her face.

But a tease? She'd never accept ownership of *that* accusation. She wasn't a tease. She might have responded to his kiss, but she hadn't initiated it, and she certainly hadn't done anything to make him believe it was going to lead to anything more.

And if he was mad because she'd ended the kiss, that was too damn bad. She'd come to her senses, realized the mistake they were making, a conclusion he would have drawn himself, if given the time. Was it her fault that she'd realized it first?

Kinda makes a guy wonder how long it's been since she's had sex.

Remembering his cutting remark, she pressed her fists against her cheeks to squeeze back the tears, the humiliation. How could he have known that about her? Had she really appeared that deprived? That *desperate*?

She rarely thought about sex or the lack of it in her life. The decision to live a nunlike existence

wasn't one she'd consciously made. It had simply…
happened. It was an instinctive means of survival
that over the years had somehow become a way of
life. A way to get over the heartbreak of losing—

She dropped her fists to her sides and squeezed
until her knuckles ached. She wouldn't think about
the past, or him. Not now. Preferably never.

But she was going to have it out with Gabe, she
told herself as she turned for her room. She wasn't
going to let him get by with calling her a tease.

Andrea Matthews might be a lot of things, but a
tease sure as heck wasn't one of them.

By the time she arrived at Gabe's cabin, it was
after three in the afternoon. Somewhere along the
drive from her house to his, she'd lost some of the
self-righteous anger that had fueled her decision
to tell him off. Now dread knotted her gut at the
thought of facing him, and she was giving serious
thought to turning around and heading back home.

But running wasn't the answer. She'd have to
deal with him sooner or later. Better to have it out
in the privacy of his home than at the station, where
every officer on duty would be able to hear what
she had to say.

Steeling herself for the confrontation, she
knocked on his front door. She waited a few moments, then knocked again and listened. But not
so much as a whisper of sound came from inside.

Frowning, she looked around. She knew he was at home, because she'd parked behind his truck.

Remembering him bragging about having all the fishing and hunting a man could want two steps out his back door, she headed toward the rear of the cabin. Beyond it stood a thick grove of trees. Since hunting season hadn't started, she doubted she'd find him there, tracking deer or other wildlife. That left the lake, which she could only assume lay on the other side of the trees. Confident that she would find him there fishing, she headed in that direction.

By the time she reached the edge of the woods, perspiration beaded her brow and dampened the back of her T-shirt. Making a mental note to tell Gabe that he'd grossly underestimated the "two steps" from his back door, she started down a faint path.

The air was cooler beneath the canopy of leaves and ripe with the scent of rotted vegetation. She drew in a deep breath, then frowned, sure that she smelled smoke, as well. Aware of the damage a fire could do in rural areas where it could destroy hundreds of acres of land before it was detected, she quickened her step. Minutes later, she reached a small clearing. In its center stood a crude, dome-shaped structure, and before it, the source of the smoke she'd smelled—a small campfire, framed by a circle of stones. More stones were piled on top of the low burning wood, making her wonder at their purpose.

"Gabe?" she called. When he didn't answer, she cautiously approached what looked to be a wickiup. Upon closer inspection, she saw that blankets draped the structure and a rectangular piece of stiffer fabric covered a low opening opposite the fire. Her curiosity piqued, she stooped to the lift the flap.

Just as she did, it flew back and Gabe appeared, his body stooped in order to clear the low opening. When he straightened, her breath caught in her lungs. His Native American heritage had never been more pronounced than at that moment. His chest was bare and gleaming with sweat, and a loincloth hung low on his hips.

Though he should have been surprised to see her, the only emotion he revealed was irritation.

"What are you doing here?"

She wiped her palms nervously down her thighs. "I—I came to talk to you."

Frowning, he hunkered down by the ring of stones and picked up a stick. "Save it for tomorrow," he said, as he poked at the fire, separating the coals. "A man's entitled to at least one day off."

"It's—it's not about work. It's…personal."

"There's nothing personal between us," he reminded her. "You've made sure of that."

"You called me a liar and a tease."

"You are."

"I'm not!" she cried angrily, then caught herself, realizing the denial was yet another lie. "Okay," she conceded. "I'll admit that I sort of enjoyed the kiss. But that doesn't make me a tease."

He spun on the balls of his feet to peer up at her. "You ended it, didn't you? You got me all stirred up, then ran like hell. In my book, that makes you a tease."

She tried to keep her gaze fixed on his face and not let it slip to his chest or, worse, to the loincloth that covered his hips. *Was he wearing anything beneath it?* Realizing the direction of her thoughts, she dug her fingernails into her palms and ordered her mind to stay focused.

"Yes, I ended it," she agreed. "I came to my senses and realized the mistake we were making. You would've realized it, too, eventually."

"I never regret kissing a beautiful woman. The mistake would be in letting the opportunity pass."

She blinked, thrown off balance for a moment by what sounded like a compliment. "We're partners," she said stubbornly. "If we became physically involved, it would destroy our ability to work together."

"How?"

The single word held enough challenge to fill her with rage.

"Because it would *end!*"

"We don't have a relationship, and you're already worrying about it ending?"

"I'm not worried. I'm stating the facts. I'm older than you. Seven years to be exact."

"So?"

"So it wouldn't work! Sooner or later the age difference would become an issue and the relationship would end!" Realizing she was all but screaming at him, she hauled in a breath. "Look," she said, forcing herself to speak more calmly, more reasonably. "I'm content with my life just the way it is. I have my job. My home. I don't want a man screwing any of that up."

"And that's what you think I would do? Screw up your life?"

"Maybe not intentionally, but, yes, I think you would."

He stood, forcing her to look up at him.

"I never took you for a coward, Andi."

"I'm not a coward."

"Yeah, you are. You're afraid of your own emotions. Scared to death to let people get too close, because you might feel something. Now that I think about it, that's probably why you're so good at your job. It's important that a detective remain emotionally detached, right? Never let his emotions interfere with a case? Hell, it's the perfect career for you."

Stunned, Andi could only stare, horrified that what he'd said might be true.

Fortunately, he didn't seem to expect a response from her. Turning, he tossed the stick into the fire. "If you want our relationship to be strictly business, I can live with that." He waited a beat, then angled his head to look at her. "But just because we can't be lovers doesn't mean we can't be friends." He extended his hand. "Right, partner?"

Andi stared at the offered hand, hesitant to take it, sure that it was a trap. But if she refused his offer of friendship, she feared he would consider it proof that she was the emotionally detached person he'd accused her of being.

Reluctantly, she placed her hand in his. "Friends," she said and shook.

Seemingly satisfied with their newly established relationship, he squatted down by the fire and picked up another stick. "I was about to take a sweat. Want to join me?"

Unfamiliar with the term, Andi frowned as she watched him shift hot rocks onto a shallow wooden bowl. "What's a sweat?"

"An old Indian tradition. A way of purifying the body, by sweating out all the impurities and toxins." He gestured behind him to the dome-shaped structure. "The sweat takes place inside the sweat lodge, the Indian's version of the modern day sauna."

"Uh...thanks, but I think I'll pass."

He set aside the stick and picked up the bowl. "It's not dangerous," he assured her as he stooped to enter the lodge. "In fact it's good for your health," he called from inside. He stuck his head out and peered up at her as he reached for the flap. "But if you don't trust yourself to be alone with me, I understand."

He dropped the flap, leaving her on the outside.

It was enough to have her whipping back the flap and ducking inside.

She stopped one step inside. The blankets covering the lodge completely blocked out the sunlight, and it took a moment for her eyes to adjust to the drastic change in lighting. When they had, she saw that Gabe was kneeling on the ground opposite her, transferring the hot stones he'd gathered to a shallow pit filled with cedar and dried grass.

"So you decided to join me."

She flattened her lips at the smugness in his tone. "Who could pass up such a gracious invitation?"

Hiding a smile, he tossed a woven mat at her feet, then sat on the opposite side of the pit and opened a hand, inviting her to sit down.

While she settled on the mat, he lifted a jug and poured water over the stones. An angry cloud of steam shot into the air as the water hissed and skipped over the hot stones.

"You'll need to take off your clothes."

Her gaze focused on the action in the pit, she snapped up her head, sure that she'd misunderstood. "What?"

"Take off your clothes. Sweats are done in the nude."

She wrapped her arms around her middle. "Thanks all the same, but I can sweat just as well with mine on."

"It's part of the ceremony," he explained. "Undergoing a sweat is a spiritual rebirth. The lodge symbolizes Mother Earth's womb. The removal of clothing is a way of shedding all our human attributes, allowing us to offer ourselves as innocent newborns to Her for cleansing and the ultimate rebirth."

She hugged her arms tighter around her body. "Well, Mother Earth will just have to use her imagination. I'm not taking off my clothes."

His expression softened to one of sympathy. "There's no reason to be ashamed of your body. I'm aware that, as a woman ages, gravity takes it toll, and certain parts of her body begin to sag."

Since his gaze had slipped to her breasts, his insinuation was clear. Insulted, she grabbed the hem of her T-shirt and ripped it over her head, then reached behind her for the hook of her bra. Holding the bra up between finger and thumb, she jutted her chin and let it drop. "You seeing anything sagging?"

He stood and reached for the leather strips that

held his loincloth in place. "No. Can't say that I do. But there's always the dreaded butt. I've heard that can drop as fast as a breast."

Andi gaped as the loincloth fell away. *Dear God,* was all she could think. She didn't know whether to pretend indifference or commend him on his excellent specimen of masculinity.

Gulping, she lifted her gaze back to his, and saw that he was watching her expectantly.

In for a penny, in for a pound, she thought with a sigh, and pushed to her feet. She stripped off her shorts, along with her panties, then quickly sat down, wadding her clothing between her legs.

He sat, too, and drizzled more water over the stones. A fresh cloud of steam rose to churn in the air, scenting it with sage and cedar. Already warm, the air became thick, making it difficult to breathe.

She lifted a hand to swipe at the perspiration that beaded her brow. "How long do we have to stay in here?" she asked impatiently.

"An hour."

"An hour!"

He pressed a finger to his lips and closed his eyes. "In order to reap the full benefits of a sweat, it must be conducted in silence."

"Benefits, my ass," Andi grumbled under her breath. "This is nothing but a way for you to get a cheap thrill."

But Gabe didn't seem to hear her complaints.

He sat in a trancelike state, with his eyes closed, his back straight as an arrow and his hands resting lightly on his spread knees. Sweat beaded on his arms and chest and rivered down his stomach to pool in the dark thatch of hair at the juncture of his legs. Heat burned her cheeks as her gaze settled on the thick column of flesh that rested against the dark nest.

Fearing he would catch her staring, she quickly looked away and pretended interest in the limbs that shaped the frame of the domed hut. But within seconds, her gaze was sliding back to the man sitting opposite her.

In the semidarkness his skin gleamed a dark bronze, his damp hair inky black. Pads of muscle shaped his chest, his abdomen, his arms. A scar that sliced low across his rib cage caught her attention and she found herself wondering how and when he'd received the wound. A souvenir from a surgery? Knifed while trying to make an arrest?

How he got the scar didn't matter, she decided. It certainly didn't detract from his looks. If anything, it added a level of danger and intrigue to an appeal she was already finding hard to resist.

She closed her eyes against the pleasure of looking at him and inhaled a deep breath, filling her lungs with steam and her senses with the scent of cedar and sage. Heat swirled around her, stroking her body like a lover's hands. Perspiration slicked her skin, but her mouth was dry as cotton. Her heart was beating too fast, and her mind was moving too slow. She tried not to think of Gabe sitting naked across from her. But awareness of his nearness became a living thing that crawled through her bloodstream and jump-kicked her nerves.

She had to get out of here, before she did something stupid, she told herself. He'd tricked her into joining him in the steam by calling her a coward. Tricked her again into taking off her clothes by insinuating that her figure was sagging. No telling what he'd try to pull next.

She had to leave. Return to the safety of her house and the world she'd created for herself there. A world with no place carved for a man. No reason for intimacy. No potential for pain.

She had one hand braced against the ground, her body poised to rise. But when she opened her eyes and found Gabe staring at her, she froze.

She found no challenge in his gaze, daring her to stay. No smugness to taunt her into continuing the sweat. She found only...heat. It stretched across the space that separated them and wound around her, binding her to that spot of ground in a way that nothing else could.

His eyes were dark, fathomless pools a woman could drown in and she was quickly going down for the third time. Her hands itched to touch him, her body burned for the touch of his.

She slowly sank back down to the mat and knotted her hand in the clothes she held on her lap. She wasn't going anywhere. Not yet, anyway.

But if anything was going to happen, it would be up to her to make the first move. She'd set the terms of their relationship when she'd told him she wasn't interested in getting physically involved with him. Insisted that it would destroy their ability to effectively work together.

He hadn't agreed, but he'd accepted her decision, said he could live with it.

Now it was up to her to convince him that he couldn't.

She drew in a shuddery breath and released it. "You said we could be friends."

He nodded.

"Have you changed your mind?"

"No. Have you?"

She shook her head, then caught her lower lip between her teeth. She had very little experience in seduction and no clue how to proceed. "D-do you think it's possible for two people to be friends and lovers at the same time?"

"Are you speaking in terms of the general population? Or did you have a particular couple in mind?"

She slanted him a frown. "I was thinking in terms of you and me."

"That would depend on our expectations. If we

entered the relationship with the understanding that it was strictly physical, and neither of us harbored a secret hope that it would develop into something more, then I don't see why it couldn't be done."

She definitely had no desire for this to develop into anything more. She wasn't even sure she could handle what she was feeling now. "I don't have a problem agreeing to those terms. Do you?"

"No."

It was the answer she'd expected and hoped for, yet he didn't make a move to approach her. Why didn't he do something? she thought in frustration. She'd all but offered herself up to him on a silver platter, yet he continued to sit there, looking at her.

"You're going to make me do this, aren't you?"

His answer was a slight curving of his lips.

Firming her jaw, she set her clothes aside and rose. Her knees trembled a bit as she rounded the pit, but she forced herself on until she reached his side. She'd thought he would at least stand to meet her. When he didn't, she shifted uneasily from foot to foot, unsure what to do next. She was an excellent marksman, could outshoot most of the men on the force. She could drop a perp to his knees with a well-placed kick or render him useless with a jab of her hand. But she had very little experience in the art of seduction.

When she continued to hesitate, he cupped a hand at her calf and lifted, guiding her leg across his. With a sigh of relief, she slowly sank down, straddling his thighs and draping her arms over his shoulders.

Now that they were sitting eye-to-eye, the heat she'd noticed in his gaze before was almost unbearable to meet. She was sure if she placed a hand in the narrow space between them, her fingers would burst into flames.

Drawing in a deep breath, she lifted her hands to frame his face and drew his mouth to hers. At the first touch of his lips, a low moan rose in her throat and her eyes shuttered closed. As they kissed, steam continued to swirl lazily around them, fed by the hot stones at her back. Lost in the arousing mist, she gave herself up to the feelings. To him.

Taste, texture, sensation. All three tangled in her mind as he slipped his tongue into her mouth to explore the secrets inside. She felt the silky glide of his hands down her back, their weight as they settled in the curve of her waist. She arched her spine at their urging, and let her head fall back, offering her throat to his lips.

With his hands now cupped at her buttocks to support her as she leaned back, he suckled and nipped a path to her chest. Her breasts ached for his touch, while her body trembled in anticipation. When at last he opened his mouth over her nipple, she dug her fingernails into his shoulders as need lanced her womb.

She'd never known this kind of hunger, this desperate desire to consume another. It was as if he'd set a wild beast loose inside her, and it now paced and clawed, looking for escape. She had to touch him, hold him or die of want.

Dragging her hands from around his neck, she smoothed them down his chest, over his hips, then brought them together to cradle his sex between her palms. She felt the shudder that moved through him, the groan that vibrated against her breast. Emboldened by his response, she stroked her fingers along his arousal, circling its tip with her thumbs. Down, then up again, she repeated the motion over and over. With each play of her hands, she felt his arousal lengthen and harden.

Another ache throbbed to life in her body, this one at the juncture of her legs. She squirmed her hips against his thighs, seeking relief. As if he sensed her need, he slipped a hand between her legs and shaped her mound. The light pressure he exerted was, at the same time, glorious and frustrating.

With a moan she touched her forehead to his. "Gabe, please," she begged.

Releasing her, he reached beside him, fumbling his hand in a pile of clothing she hadn't noticed before. When he drew it out, he held a gold-foil disk.

She stared in amazement as he opened it and

rolled a condom into place. "Are you always this prepared?" she asked in disbelief.

He tossed aside the wrapper. "I'm a Boy Scout. I'm *always* prepared." He shifted her on his lap, aligning her hips with his, then lifted a brow. "But if you'd rather take your chances with Russian Roulette, I can take it off."

She shook her head. "No. I was just surprised."

Nodding, he slipped his hands beneath her hips. "If you're having any second thoughts, this might be the time to voice them."

She locked her hands around his neck. "I'm not."

With another nod, he pushed inside.

The first thrust left Andi gasping. The second elicited a low, guttural groan. By the third, she was braced up on her knees, catching the rhythm and riding him hard. Her breathing became ragged; her muscles burned from the exertion. Pressure built inside her, gathering into an unbearable knot of need in her womb.

Squeezing her eyes shut, she arched, searching for the release that danced maddeningly just out of her reach. "Gabe, please," she begged pitifully.

He set his jaw. "Together," he said, then pulled her hips hard against his.

His body went rigid and she felt the quivering strain of muscle, the shudders that moved through him. At last the knot inside her exploded, a shattering release of sensation and emotion that shot her high, sending wave after wave of pleasure rippling through her body.

Gradually she became aware of the hand at the middle of her back, the sensation of falling as Gabe sank back to the ground, drawing her with him. Then she was nestled against his chest, his heart a hammer beneath her ear, his arms holding her close.

"You okay?"

Fascinated by the sharp ridge of his collarbone, she stroked a finger lazily along its length. "What's your definition of okay?"

A chuckle rumbled through his chest. "If you can talk, that's good enough for me."

Feeling rather smug, she pushed a toe down the length of his leg. "How often do you take these sweats?"

He lifted his head to look at her. "Who said this one was over?"

Smiling, she inched her way up his chest and pressed her lips to his. "I was hoping you'd say that."

Andi awoke, cocooned by an unaccustomed warmth. She opened her eyes and blinked at the branches that framed the wall of the dome-shaped structure, then at the now cold stones that lay in the shallow pit on the ground before her. It took a moment for her to realize where she was. Another to identify the source of heat spooned at her back.

It took half that time for the regrets to set in.

She glanced over her shoulder and saw that Gabe was still asleep. Hoping to escape before he awoke, she braced an elbow against the ground and started to rise. A hand on her hip stopped her.

"Where're you going?" he asked sleepily.

"Home. It's getting late."

He slid his hand to her belly and drew her hips back to cradle against his groin. "Not that late."

"I—I've got things to do."

"Like what?"

She searched her brain for a viable excuse to offer. "I—I need to water my yard."

He nuzzled her neck and rolled his hips suggestively against hers. "Water it tomorrow."

She could feel herself weakening and quickly rolled away from him and to her feet. "Can't," she said as she grabbed her shorts and tugged them on. "Thanks for the…sweat."

He lifted himself up on an elbow. "Andi," he said quietly, "don't run away."

"I'm not," she insisted, avoiding his gaze. She pulled her T-shirt over her head, then reached for her tennis shoes. "I've…I've just got things to do."

"Nothing's changed," he warned her. "We can be partners and lovers, too."

"Yeah," she said, then stooped to duck through

the low opening, desperate to escape before she succumbed to temptation again. "Whatever you say."

Andi's nerves were pretty much shot by the time she made it back to town. In the space of one afternoon she'd broken every rule she'd ever made for herself and placed her career in jeopardy.

"Stupid, stupid, stupid," she cried softly, emphasizing each repetition with a slap of her hand against the steering wheel. She knew better than to get involved with a co-worker. Relationships ended, and when they did, few people survived the awkwardness and bad feelings that sometimes remained after a breakup. She knew that, yet, she'd consciously ignored the danger and made love with Gabe.

What she'd done was stupid. Foolish. Crazy!

She turned onto her driveway, shoved the gearshift into Park, then lowered her head to the steering wheel with a moan.

And if she had it to do over again, she'd probably do the same dang thing.

She'd enjoyed it. Every moment. And she'd probably be enjoying more of the same at this very minute if her common sense hadn't finally decided to surface.

But she couldn't let it happen again. Wouldn't. The one thing she'd learned from the experience was that it could be addicting. She'd enjoyed having sex with Gabe way too much to allow herself to repeat the experience. If she did, she might begin to depend on him, even *need* him, and she refused to let anyone or anything have that much control over her life.

With a sigh, she lifted her head and reached for her purse. She froze, her gaze locked on her closed garage door. Painted in bright red, the word *whore* screamed at her from the door's front panels. Numb, she got out of her car and stood before the door, sickened by the vandalism as much as she was by the word itself.

Who would do such a thing to her? she asked in disbelief. Granted, law enforcement officers received more than their share of grief from the public they served. Eggs splattered over their vehicles. Obscenities shouted in their faces. But this seemed more than a petty grievance aimed at someone who wore a badge. The word itself seemed to make it personal.

Heat crawled up her neck as she remembered the way she'd spent her afternoon and evening. Was it a coincidence that someone had chosen this particular day to spray graffiti on her garage door? Or had the person known she was with Gabe?

Ice slid through her veins. No, she told herself, and stiffened her spine, refusing to believe that was the case. There was no way anyone could've known she was going to Gabe's. She hadn't planned to go. It was an impulsive decision she'd made minutes before leaving her house for his.

But the irony of someone choosing to paint *whore* on her garage on the very day that she'd broken her vow of celibacy was a little hard for her to swallow. The sexual implication alone made her question whether the word was chosen at random. Added to that was the fact that the vandal had struck while she wasn't at home. Another coincidence? Not likely, since Sunday was the day she usually spent working around her house.

When considered individually, each of the factors could be deemed coincidental. But when they were combined, it was clear that whoever had painted the graffiti not only knew she was away from home but knew where she was and exactly what she was doing.

Richard?

She turned her gaze to her neighbor's house. He, better than anyone else, would know her comings and goings. Her driveway was in clear view of his living room window, as well as the one in his kitchen.

But how would he have known she was at Gabe's?

The hair on the back of her neck prickled. There was only one way he could've known.

He had followed her.

Chapter 5

Ryan Fortune stood before the window in his office at Fortune TX, Ltd. staring out at the manicured grounds that surrounded the office complex. Though he'd turned over the controls of the company to his nephew and now only served in an advisory capacity, he'd kept his office and enjoyed his visits to headquarters, as they allowed him to keep up with the company's operations. The pain in his head was almost blinding and seemed to increase with each passing day. There were times when he wondered if it wasn't a physical malady he suffered, but a punishment from God. Though he'd tried to live a good and honorable life, he harbored secrets that shamed him…and haunted him.

Linda Faraday topped the list.

He rubbed at his temple, the thought of her seeming to make his head ache even more.

He knew he should bring Linda and her son into the Fortune family. He'd kept their existence a secret for much too long. But the decision to do so wasn't a selfish one. He'd wanted only to protect the memory of his brother, Cameron. If he brought Linda and her son into the family, he'd have to explain her appearance, and everyone would know that Cameron had embezzled millions of dollars from Fortune TX, Ltd., a crime that Linda, as an undercover operative for the government, had been assigned to prove.

Unfortunately for her, Linda had fallen in love with Cameron and made the mistake of climbing into a car with him when he was drunk. The automobile accident that had ensued had cost Cameron his life and had left Linda in a kind of coma. Seven months later, while still locked in a coma, she had given birth to a son. Cameron's son.

The government hadn't wanted to jeopardize Linda's identity as an operative and had protected her by making it appear that she, too, had died in the accident, when in fact she had lain in a coma for over ten years.

It was through his own government contacts that Ryan had discovered the cover-up and learned of

Linda's existence. And it was that knowledge that now haunted him.

He squeezed his head between his hands, trying to still the painful throbbing, to block out the haunting memories, the guilt. He supposed it was the discovery of the body in Lake Mondo that had made him think of Linda, of Cameron.

The crown-shaped birthmark on the victim's hip suggested that the dead man was a Fortune, but when called upon to identify the body, Ryan hadn't recognized the man.

He dropped his hands to his sides, with a weary sigh. Now he had yet another worry to add to the long list of troubles he faced.

Had Cameron fathered another son, before his death?

"Mr. Fortune, have you got a minute?"

Ryan turned, then smiled, when he saw Jason Wilkes standing in the doorway to his office. He was rather proud of Jason's accomplishments since coming on board Fortune TX, Ltd., especially since he'd pushed so hard for the young man to be hired. Jason had proved himself to be a hard worker and was showing great promise. "Sure, Jason. Come on in."

"Are you okay?" Jason asked as he entered. "You look a little pale."

Ryan waved away the concern. "I'm fine. Just a little tired. What can I do for you?"

"I had wanted to review these spreadsheets with you. But if you're tired, it can wait."

Ryan shook his head and settled behind his desk. "Now is as good a time as any. Show me what you've got."

Andi stormed into the station, looking as if she were primed for a fight. It didn't take her long to find one.

"Hey, Andi," Reynolds called. "How 'bout having dinner with me tonight?" The officer was nothing if not persistent. And annoying.

She spun on a dime, slapped her hands down on his desk and shoved her face up to his. "The answer is no, Reynolds, and will continue to be no, no matter how many times you ask. Understand?"

He lifted his hands. "Hey. I was just joking around."

She pushed away from his desk. "Do you see me laughing?"

Dumbfounded, Reynolds watched her stalk away, then glanced over at Gabe. "What's up with her?"

Wondering the same thing himself, Gabe pushed to his feet. "I don't know, but I intend to find out."

When he reached the break room, he found Andi standing before the coffeemaker, her hands gripped around a coffee mug, as if it were somebody's throat.

"Strangling it won't improve the taste."

With a scowl, she slammed the mug down on the counter and turned away. "Mind your own damn business."

"Whoa," he said, and caught her arm as she stormed past him. "What's wrong with you?"

"I'm in a lousy mood, okay? So buzz off."

This was more than a lousy mood and Gabe knew it. The dark circles beneath her eyes indicated a sleepless night, and there was only one reason he could think of that could have caused it. "If it's about what happened yesterday..." he began.

She jerked free and glared at him. "Not everything is about *you,* Thunderhawk."

Though the urge to snap back at her was strong, Gabe managed to suppress it. "I'm your partner. What affects you, affects me."

"So deal with it."

He caught her elbow and shoved her ahead of him toward a table. "Apology accepted."

She tried to twist free. "That wasn't an apology."

"Close enough." He pushed her down onto a chair, then hitched his hip on the table's edge, successfully boxing her in. "Start talking."

She dropped her forehead to her hands and dug her fingers through her hair. "Someone vandalized my house last night while I was gone."

He heard the anger in her voice, and below it a thread of something else. Fear?

"How did they get inside?"

She dropped her hands with a weary sigh and sank back against the chair. "It wasn't a break-in. Some jerk painted graffiti on my garage door."

"Do you know who's responsible?"

She opened her hands. "Can you believe my luck? My first original piece of artwork, and the artist forgets to sign his name."

He ignored her sarcasm. "Did you talk to your neighbors? They might have seen or heard something."

She snorted a laugh and dragged the rubber band from her ponytail. "Yeah, I talked to them." She scraped back her hair, holding the thick shank she gathered in one hand, while wrapping the band back into place with the other. "They're already organizing a Neighborhood Watch meeting."

He stood and pulled her to her feet. "Let's go."

She stumbled along at his side. "Where?"

"Your place."

Andi didn't want Gabe nosing around her house, but trying to stop him was like trying to stop a bulldozer on a downhill course.

He dusted the garage door for prints, did a complete sweep of her front and backyard and even climbed up on her roof. When none of those things produced any evidence, he returned to the driveway and stood before the brown construction paper she'd used to cover up the graffiti.

"Mind if I take a look?" he asked.

Though she knew he wouldn't find any clues to her vandal's identity there, either, she stood back and watched while he peeled back the duct tape.

As the paper fell away, exposing the word *whore,* she set her jaw and waited for his reaction, silently praying he wouldn't make the same associations she had when she'd first seen the word.

When he remained silent, staring, she dropped her arms and snatched the paper up from the drive. "Talented guy, huh?" she said as she slapped the paper over the door, covering up the vandal's work. "A real Picasso."

Gabe closed a hand over her wrist. "Where do you keep your paint?"

She shot him a frown. "If you think I'm stupid enough to leave cans of spray paint lying around for some idiot to steal, you're wrong."

"That wasn't what I was suggesting. I want the paint that was originally used on the door."

Firming her lips, she whacked a fist against the duct tape, pressing it back into place. "No way. You're not painting my garage door."

He unbuttoned a cuff and began rolling up his sleeves. "Try and stop me."

It was hard enough for Andi to allow someone to do something for her that she was more than capable of doing herself. But to stand around and watch him do it required more stamina than she possessed.

So while Gabe repainted her garage door, she hid inside her house and passed the time by surfing the Internet for mention of a missing person bearing a crown-shaped birthmark. One-by-one she clicked the links produced by the search engine. She had eliminated three screens worth of possibilities when she heard the back door open and Gabe call, "Andi?"

Still peeved with him, she called irritably, "In here!"

She glanced over her shoulder as he entered the room, bringing with him the scent of fresh paint and the stronger, more pungent odor of paint thinner.

He stopped behind her chair and looked over her shoulder as he buttoned his cuffs at his wrists. "What are you doing?"

She reached for the mouse to click another link. "Searching the Internet for our Lost Fortune."

"Find anything?"

"Not yet." Another screen popped up and she began to scan the newspaper article that appeared.

Gabe dragged up a stool and positioned it beside her chair. "We need to talk," he said as he sat down.

Her attention focused on the article she was reading, she said distractedly, "About what?"

"The graffiti."

She tensed, but kept her gaze on the screen. "What about it?"

"I don't think this was random. Whoever did this meant it as a message."

"Since I'm the only person living here, I suppose that message was meant for me."

"So it would seem. And since you're an employee of the police department, it would be natural to assume the message was spawned by something you did in the line of work, rather than directed at you as a person."

"Yeah," she agreed hesitantly. "So?"

"So why the word *whore?* Pig. Skunk. Even bitch, I could understand. Whore just doesn't make sense."

"Vandalism seldom does," she replied evasively.

"You're not a promiscuous woman, Andi."

She swallowed, but still couldn't find the courage to look at him. "You've got to quit with these compliments, Gabe."

He shot to his feet. "Would you quit with the sarcasm? This is serious."

"Would you rather I scream and cry? Sorry. That's not my style."

He turned away with a sigh and dragged a hand over his hair. "I think I know who did this."

Stunned, she spun her chair around. "Who?"

"Deirdre."

She stared, then choked a laugh. "Come on, Gabe. Deirdre's my friend. If she had something to say to me, she'd say it to my face. She wouldn't need to spray it in Krylon on my garage door."

"What if the message wasn't for you? What if it was revenge against me?"

She bit her lower lip, remembering the warning about Gabe that Deirdre had offered in the break room. *He's a user.... I've got the footprints to prove it.*

"I wouldn't put it past her," he went on. "She's been hassling me ever since I broke things off with her. Following me around town. Leaving notes on my truck. Calling my house all hours of the night and hanging up."

She thought of the hang-up calls she'd received during the last month, then shook off the doubts that were rising, refusing to believe that Deirdre would do anything so juvenile or petty.

She spun her chair back around to face the screen. "Sorry, Gabe," she said as she searched for the point where she'd stopped reading. "But your ego is showing. Deirdre isn't pining away for you like you think. She's got a new man in her life. She told me so herself."

"Then how do you—"

A phrase seemed to leap at her from the screen and she held up a hand, silencing him. "Listen," she said, and began reading. "'Elizabeth DuBois, wife of the missing man, describes her husband as five-ten, weighing approximately one hundred and seventy-five pounds and bearing a crown-shaped mark on his hip. Anyone with information concerning the whereabouts of Chad DuBois should call the New Orleans Police Department at blah, blah, blah....'"

She spun her chair around. "This could be our floater! The Lost Fortune!"

"Maybe," he said hesitantly as he crossed to look at the screen. After reading the information, he straightened, shaking his head. "That article is two weeks old."

"So? Our floater's been around for over two *months*." She leaped from the chair, flung her arms around his neck, then charged for the door.

"Pack your bags, Thunderhawk," she called over her shoulder. "We're going to Louisiana!"

By the time they landed in New Orleans, it was after ten at night. Planning to pay a visit to Mrs. DuBois the next morning, they rented a car and drove to a hotel.

After parking, Gabe grabbed their bags and led the way into the lobby. He dropped the bags by the front desk. "We need a room for the night," he told the clerk.

"Queen or a king?"

Stifling a yawn, he reached in his back pocket for his wallet. "King."

An elbow rammed his ribs.

He shot Andi a frown. "What the hell was that for?"

She burned him with a look, then said to the desk clerk, "Make that *two* kings."

The clerk eyed them curiously as he adjusted his computer screen. "I'll check availability." He studied the screen a moment, then smiled. "It appears we have two adjoining kings on the fifth floor."

Gabe dropped his credit card on the counter. "Fine. We'll take 'em."

Andi shoved her card next to his. "Put the charges for my room on my card."

The man looked at Gabe, as if unsure what to do.

"Do as the lady says," he said wearily. "She's the boss."

After signing his credit slip and receiving his key, Gabe picked up his bag and headed for the elevator. He punched the button, then looked up at the floor indicator, watching the car's slow descent.

Andi joined him seconds later. "Are you crazy?" she whispered angrily. "If we had turned in an expense voucher for only one room, everybody at the station would think we're having an affair."

"Well, aren't we?"

She opened her mouth to reply, but closed it when she saw that the desk clerk was watching their exchange with obvious interest.

The elevator doors swished open.

"We'll talk about this later," she said under her breath, then stepped inside.

When Gabe didn't follow, she slapped a hand against the door to keep it from closing. "Well?" she asked impatiently. "Are you coming or not?"

He stared at her a long moment, then turned away. "Not."

Dressed for bed, Andi paced her hotel room, listening for a sound from the room next door. She stopped to glance at her wristwatch and groaned when she saw that it was after two in the morning.

And still no sign of Gabe.

Where could he have gone? she asked herself for the hundredth time since arriving at her room. Surely he wouldn't have left town without her?

Remembering the look on his face in the lobby before he'd turned and walked away, she sank to the side of the bed and covered her face with her hands. She should have told him before they left town that she had no intention of continuing their affair. If she had, they could've avoided that whole ugly scene in the lobby. But she'd been so caught up with the prospect of finally putting closure on the Lost Fortune case, she hadn't thought of anything else.

A sound came from the hallway.

She dropped her hands and straightened, listening, sure that she had heard movement in the room next to hers. Hurrying to the door that joined her room to Gabe's, she twisted it open, then knocked on the inner door that opened from his room. "Gabe?" she called hesitantly. "Is that you?"

She waited, listening, then knocked again, louder. "Gabe?"

She lifted her hand to knock a third time, but the door swung open.

She slowly lowered her hand. "Where have you been? I was worried."

Scowling, he turned away, stripping off his shirt. "I'm a big boy. I can take care of myself."

Determined to set things straight between them, she strode into his room. "We need to talk."

He snatched a hanger from the closet rod and draped his shirt over it. "No need. I got the message loud and clear. You don't want anyone to know that we've slept together." He hooked the hanger over the rod, then reached for his belt. "You've got my word. Your secret is safe with me."

"Dammit, Gabe," she said in frustration. "You make it sound like I'm ashamed of you or something."

He glanced her way and lifted a brow. "Well, aren't you? You do outrank me," he reminded her. "I'm sure sleeping with a lowly police officer must be like slumming for a detective. And there is that problem with the difference in our ages," he went on, then stopped to scratch his head. "But now that I think about it, shouldn't snagging a younger man be something an older woman would want to brag about, not hide?"

She felt the tears rising and stubbornly fought them back.

He snapped his fingers. "Wait. I know what the problem is. It's because I'm a Native American, isn't it? You're probably one of those racists who thinks Indians should still be locked up on reservations. It's okay to sleep with one, but you sure as hell wouldn't want to be seen with one."

She clapped her hands over her ears. "Why are you saying these things?" she cried. "Is it to hurt me? To get even with me because I hurt you?" She let her hands fall to her sides, suddenly too tired to fight with him any longer. "Well, if that's the case, you've succeeded. We're even. There's no need to say any more."

She turned for the adjoining door.

"So that's it? It's over?"

She stopped, her hand on the knob, knowing he was referring to more than their argument.

"I told you it wouldn't work."

"It was working just fine for me."

She whirled to face him. "Well, it wasn't for me."

"I don't remember hearing any complaints from you while we were making love yesterday."

She curled her hands into fists at her sides.

"No, but I've had an affair before. I know what can happen when it ends. I won't go through that kind of pain again."

"So that's it," he said, turning away. "I get to pay for someone else's mistake." He glanced back to look at her. "Was it someone I know? One of the guys at the station?"

"No. It was a long time ago. A college professor."

"Did he dump you?"

She set her jaw and swung around, intending to leave. "That's none of your business."

He lunged and caught her arm. "I think it is. If I'm going to pay for the guy's mistakes, I should at least know what he did to you."

She pulled free. "He was fired, all right? It was against university rules for a professor to date a student, and he lost his job."

"I'd think a professor would be smart enough to know to be discreet."

"He *was* smart. A genius, in fact. My roommate found out about us and told one of the deans."

"Your roommate ratted you out? Man, that's low."

The memory of the hurt, the betrayal she'd experienced at the hands of someone whom she'd thought was her best friend wasn't something Andi would ever forget. "You don't know the half of it."

"Did you continue to see each other after he lost his job?"

She turned away. "He left town."

"Why didn't you go with him? You obviously loved the guy."

"He didn't ask. I went to his apartment one afternoon and he was…gone."

"And you think I'd do the same thing."

It wasn't a question, but a statement, yet she felt he deserved some kind of response.

"I don't know that you would." She turned to face him. "But I can't take the chance. I won't go through that again. I can't."

He blew out a breath. "Wow. You really know how to make a guy feel like a jerk, don't you?"

"That wasn't my intent."

"Yeah, I know." He cupped his hands on her shoulders. "I told you we could be friends." When she lowered her gaze, he placed his thumbs beneath her chin, forcing her to look at him. "I won't lie and say I'm not disappointed, but I'm still your friend. Whether we're lovers or not doesn't change that."

That he would still want to be her friend, after the angry words they'd exchanged, after all she'd told him, touched her in a way that little else could. "I could use a friend right now."

"I'd imagine you could've used one then."

Tears filled her eyes at the truth in the statement.

Her best and *only* friend at the time had been her roommate, the person who was responsible for ruining her life and that of the man she loved. "More than you'll ever know."

He slid an arm around her shoulder and drew her with him to his bed. "Enough talk for one night. Let's go to bed."

At her stunned looked, he held up his hands. "Nothing sexual, I swear. Consider me your personal teddy bear. Your security blanket. Whatever you need me to be, that's what I am."

He pulled back the covers, guided her beneath them, then switched off the bedside lamp. In the darkness, she heard the scrape of his zipper, felt the mattress dip as he sat down on the edge of the bed and pulled off his slacks. A moment later, he was lifting the covers and sliding into bed beside her.

He slipped an arm beneath her head and leaned over to press a kiss to her forehead. "Good night, Andi."

Then he laid his head on the pillow next to hers and closed his eyes.

Figuring this was just another ruse to get her into bed with him, she waited for him to try something, ready to slug him when he did. One minute passed. Two. She glanced his way with a frown. Three minutes. Four. Realizing by his rhythmic breathing that he was asleep, she slowly relaxed her tense muscles and curled up against him.

* * *

When Andi awakened, she was lying on her side and Gabe was spooned against her back, his left arm draped over her hip. It was the same position she'd found herself in when she'd awakened in his sweat lodge. She waited for the panic to set in, but oddly, it never did. She felt safe, secure, even comforted by his nearness, which was weird, to say the least.

The guy was a paradox. She hadn't believed for a minute, when he'd tucked her into bed, that he intended to just sleep with her. She'd thought for sure the teddy bear/security blanket offer was just another ruse.

But he hadn't tried anything. He'd dropped a kiss on her forehead, said good-night, then gone to sleep. Nothing sexual, he'd promised. And he'd kept his word. She should be ecstatic, relieved.

So why was she disappointed?

His nose bumped the curve of her neck, and she tensed.

"Good mornin'," he said sleepily.

Here it comes, she thought, holding her breath. The seduction she'd expected.

But instead of snuggling up to her, he flung himself up from the bed, stretched his arms to the ceiling, then dropped them with a sigh and headed for the shower.

"Hope you're planning on having breakfast," he called over his shoulder. "I'm starving."

By all appearances, Chad and Elizabeth DuBois were living the quintessential middle-class existence. Two-story brick home, with a well-groomed yard and an SUV parked in the drive.

Andi wondered how long Mrs. DuBois would be able to continue her current lifestyle if her husband turned out to be Lost Fortune.

"Let me do the talking," she told Gabe as she pressed the doorbell.

He nodded. "You're the boss."

She drew in a breath, mentally preparing herself to deal with an hysterical female.

The door opened, and a woman stepped into the space.

"Mrs. DuBois?" Andi asked.

"Yes. I'm Elizabeth DuBois."

Andi flashed her badge. "I'm Detective Matthews with the Red Rock, Texas, police department, and this," she said, indicating Gabe, "is my partner, Officer Thunderhawk."

"I've been expecting you. Sergeant Maxwell called to tell me you were coming."

"If you can spare us a few minutes, we'd like to ask you a few questions."

Mrs. DuBois opened the door wider. "Of course. I'm sorry. Please come in."

Andi and Gabe followed her into the living room. She picked up a remote and switched off the television, then gestured to the sofa. "You're from Texas?" she said as she perched on the edge of the chair opposite them.

Andi nodded. "Yes, ma'am. Officer Thunderhawk and I have been working on a case and we're hoping you could answer some questions for us."

"Chad isn't in any trouble, is he?"

"None that we're aware of," Andi replied evasively, then cleared her throat. "How long has your husband been missing?"

Tears filled her eyes and she reached to pull a tissue from a box on the coffee table. "Almost four months now."

"Why did you wait so long to file a missing person report?"

Mrs. DuBois ducked her head, as if embarrassed. "This isn't the first time he's done this," she admitted. "Left me, I mean." She dabbed at her eyes. "Chad has…problems. I wasn't aware of them when we first married. He hides them very well. It wasn't until after we'd been married several years that I began to suspect something was wrong."

She took a deep breath, then continued. "His job required him to travel, but his out-of-town trips seemed to increase. Then I discovered money missing from our account. I questioned him about it and he was evasive. When I persisted, he became angry. Even violent.

"I thought at first he was having an affair, so I hired a private detective." She shuddered at the memory. "The man obviously wasn't very good at his job, because Chad knew immediately that he was being followed. He confronted me about it, threatened that if I ever did anything like that again, he would divorce me."

She opened her hands on her lap in a helpless gesture. "There's no way I could support myself and my children. I have no skills, no college education." She dropped her chin. "So I stayed."

"You said you *thought* he was having an affair," Andi pressed. "Were you never able to prove it?"

She shook her head. "No. But I believe it's more than that. I'm afraid that Chad is connected with drugs in some way. Maybe a dealer. In the months before he disappeared, he received several phone calls late at night and he would get up and dress and leave. He claimed that it was someone at the company who had called and that there was a crisis that only he could handle."

She shook her head again. "But I didn't believe him. One night, after he returned and had gone back to bed, I snuck out to the garage and went through his car. I found a gun in his glove box and a duffel bag full of money in his trunk."

The more the woman talked, the more plausible

it seemed to Andi that Chad could have ended up as fish bait in Lake Mondo. Eager to verify the connection that would identify Chad as their floater, she pulled a copy of the newspaper article from her pocket. "You were quoted in this article as saying your husband has a crown-shaped mark on his hip."

She shuddered. "Yes, and it was disgusting. Chad's nickname is King," she went on to explain. "His fraternity brothers started calling him that in college and still do to this day. Several years ago, a couple of them were in town for Mardi Gras and invited Chad to join them in the French Quarter for a few beers. Although, it turned out to be more than a few," she added bitterly. "Chad was pretty much wasted by the time he got home.

"Anyway, they were walking down the street and one of the guys—Bill, I think—saw a tattoo parlor. One thing led to another and they all three ended up inside. Chad knew how I felt about tattoos. They are so white trash, if you know what I mean. He really didn't care for them, either.

"I don't believe he would've gotten one on his own, but with his buddies there egging him on, I'm sure he didn't want to look like a coward. Bill and Justin had their arms tattooed with an eagle. Thankfully Chad asked the artist to put his on his rear end. A crown," she added. "His buddies are the ones who chose the design, not Chad. They said that every 'king' should have his own crown."

Andi's heart sank. "So the crown on your husband's hip was a tattoo, not a birthmark?"

Mrs. DuBois looked at her curiously. "Well, yes. Why?"

Andi tried her best to hide her disappointment, as she rose. "I'm sorry, Mrs. DuBois. But the man we're looking for has a crown-shaped birthmark on his hip, not a tattoo."

Mrs. DuBois rose slowly, her eyes filling with tears. "So you don't know where my husband is?"

Andi shook her head. "No, ma'am. I'm sorry."

Chapter 6

As Gabe pulled up in front of Andi's house, her cell phone beeped, signaling the receipt of a text message.

"I swear Joe has radar trained on me," she grumbled as she pulled the phone from the clip at her waist. "My plane barely hits the ground, and he's already tracked me down."

Gabe switched on the overhead dome light and waited while she checked the message, knowing that if it was a dispatch from the station he'd be going, as well. "So?" he prodded when she didn't say anything. "Where are we headed?"

She quickly flipped down the phone cover and

shook her head as she clipped it back at her waist. "It— The message wasn't from Joe."

"Who was it from, then?"

She shook her head again and reached for her purse. "Nobody. It wasn't important."

Frowning, Gabe plucked the phone from her waist. "Try telling that to someone who'll believe it."

"Hey!" Andi cried, reaching for her phone.

Gabe put up an arm, blocking her, while he read the message on the screen. *Welcome home, Andi. How was New Orleans?* He set his jaw, understanding now why she hadn't wanted him to see the message. "No one but department certified personnel has this cell number."

Scowling, she snatched the phone from his hand. "Yeah," she muttered as she clipped it back at her waist. "It's amazing how technologically superior deviates are these days."

When she reached over the seat for her bag, Gabe clamped a hand over her arm. "No way are you staying here. You're going home with me."

She jerked free. "I'm not letting some creep scare me away from my own house."

"Fine." He reached over the seat and snatched up his bag. "Then I'll stay with you."

"No!"

Ignoring her, he climbed down from his truck and headed down the sidewalk for her front door.

In the Arms of the Law

A door slammed behind him. "You're *not* staying here," she said furiously as she ran to catch up.

He clucked his tongue and stepped aside, giving her room to deal with the lock. "Do you really want to create a scene in front of your neighbors?"

Curling her lip in a snarl, she unlocked the door. Gabe quickly moved in behind her and nudged her across the threshold.

"Got any beer?" he asked as he dropped his bag to the floor.

"You're not staying."

With a shrug, he headed for the kitchen. "Looks to me like I am."

He opened the refrigerator door and smiled as he pulled out a beer. "Ah. My favorite brand."

"Good. Enjoy it on the way home."

He popped the top. "It's against the law to drink and drive."

The doorbell rang.

She flattened her lips in irritation at the interruption. "As soon as you finish that beer," she warned him as she headed for the door, "you're out of here."

"Hey, gorgeous," Gabe heard a man say. "Where've you been? I haven't seen you around in a couple of days."

Gorgeous? Frowning, Gabe peeked into the hall. Whoa, he thought, trying not to laugh when he saw the man standing opposite Andi. If his sisters-in-law saw this guy, fashion tickets would be flying.

Bleached blond hair. Gold chain around the throat. The clincher, though, was the silk shirt he wore unbuttoned halfway to his waist.

Gabe wasn't sure what made him do it, but he ripped his T-shirt over his head, shot his fingers through his hair, spiking it, and headed for the door.

"Honey, what's the holdup?" he called, then stopped and winced. "Oops, sorry," he said, and continued on to the door. "I didn't realize we had company." Smiling, he draped an arm over Andi's shoulders and stuck out his hand to the visitor. "Hi, I'm Gabe."

The guy looked at Gabe as if he was a fly that had just landed in his soup. "Richard Givens, Andi's neighbor."

"Richard Givens?" Gabe repeated. "As in Givens Motors?" He glanced at Andi. "Honey, why didn't you tell me you had someone famous living right next door?" He turned back to Richard. "Why, I bet your picture's in the paper more often than the mayor's. Of course, yours is always attached to one of your ads. But, hey," he said, opening a hand, "fame is fame, even if you do have to pay for it, right, buddy?"

His face mottled with fury, Richard spun on a heel and stalked away.

Gabe stepped out onto the porch. "Hey, what's the rush?" he called after him. "Stick around. We'll have a beer."

Richard kept walking, but shot his middle finger in the air, letting Gabe know what he thought of his invitation.

With a shrug, Gabe closed the door. "I guess he had other plans."

"I can't believe you did that."

He looked at her incredulously. "I'd think you'd thank me for getting rid of him. Hell, did you see that shirt? I've seen pimps with better fashion sense."

"If you'd minded your own business, I could've found out if he was the one who left the message."

"You think Richard Givens is the guy who's been hassling you?" he asked, unable to believe the man was intelligent enough to pull off a stunt like that.

"He has opportunity, motive and—"

He held up a hand. "Wait a minute. Opportunity I can see. He lives next door. But what grievance could he possibly have with you? Does your dog do its business in his yard?"

Rolling her eyes, she pushed past him. "I don't have a dog."

"See?" he said, following her to the kitchen. "No motive."

"I won't go out with him, all right?" She snatched up his T-shirt and threw it at him. "He asks all the time, and I keep turning him down."

"So he spray paints *whore* on your garage door to get back at you?" He pulled the T-shirt over his head. "If that's what you're basing your assumption on, every single guy at the station would be a suspect, me included." He pulled out a chair at the table and plucked a napkin from the holder. "Got a pen?"

"You're leaving, remember?"

"No, I'm making a suspect list."

Heaving a sigh, she pulled a pen from a drawer and tossed it to him.

"Richard. Deirdre." He scrawled the names on the napkins, then looked up. "Who else?"

"Strike Deirdre's name."

"Why?"

"She has an alibi. The night my garage was spray painted she was on duty."

"She could've dropped by here while on patrol, done the dirty work, then gone on about her business. The name stays. Who else?"

"I don't know," she said wearily. "I just want to go to bed."

"Okay," he said, frowning at the names. "I'll be there in a minute."

"You're not sleeping with me."

"You've got a guest room, don't you?"

"Yes, but—"

"Fine. I'll bunk in there."

Usually within five minutes of hitting the sheets, Andi was asleep. But tonight she lay wide-eyed, listening to the sounds of Gabe moving about. She wasn't accustomed to having anyone in her house and each sound he made, no matter how slight, sounded like a bomb going off.

She heard yet another thump, Gabe's muffled curse, then footsteps in the hall. Her bedroom door opened slowly with a creak of hinges.

"Andi? You asleep?"

She pushed up to her elbows. "No. Thanks to you, I'm wide-awake."

The overhead light flashed on, and she threw up a hand to shade her eyes. "Gabe!"

"Sorry."

The light blinked off and he crossed to stand beside the bed. "Move over. And before you start bitchin' and moanin', I should remind you that the bed in your guest room is not a real bed. A midget wouldn't fit in that matchbox. And don't bother suggesting the sofa. I already tried and have a crick in my neck to prove it."

Rolling her eyes, she flipped back the covers. "Oh, for heaven's sake. Get in, so I can get some sleep."

He crawled into the bed, spent a moment plumping the pillow and adjusting the covers, then settled beside her with a contented sigh. "Good night, Andi."

She punched her pillow. "You're going home tomorrow."

"Uh-huh," he said vaguely.

"I mean it. I don't need or want you here. I can take care of myself."

He rolled to his side and draped an arm across her middle. "So you keep saying." He snuggled his head next to hers on her pillow. "'Night, Andi."

Gabe strode into the police station the next morning and crossed straight to Chief Prater's office. "I need to talk to you, sir."

Prater looked at him curiously, then waved him in. "What's the problem?"

"It's Andi. Someone's stalking her." He laid out the events of the previous days, with Prater listening intently, the ever present cigar clamped between his teeth. He ended with the text message she'd received upon their return from Louisiana.

Prater snatched the cigar from his mouth. "Where is she? And why the hell hasn't she told me about this before?"

"She's on her way in now." Gabe raised a brow. "And I think you know why she hasn't said anything."

"Muleheaded woman," Prater grumbled. "Thinks she can handle everything herself." He tried to hide a smile, his pride in his detective, as well as his affection for her, obvious. "Gutsiest broad I've ever met. Took a chance when I hired her on as detective. The first female ever to hold the position on the Red Rock force. She's never once given me reason to regret that decision."

"She's a good detective," Gabe agreed.

Frowning, the chief reared back in his chair and studied Gabe, once again clutching the cigar between his teeth. "Do you think this has anything to do with the Lost Fortune case?"

Gabe shook his head. "I don't think so. But it could be someone she's dealt with before, some perp she's put behind bars."

"So what do you suggest we do about it?"

"I intend to keep an eye on her twenty-four seven. I stayed with her last night and—"

The chief shot to his feet and snatched the cigar from his mouth. "You did *what?*"

Gabe held up his hands. "For protection only. And believe me," he added, "she kicked up a pretty good fuss about it."

The chief choked a laugh and sat back down. "I'd have liked to have seen that. She doesn't take to pampering or coddling."

"No," Gabe agreed. "She's tough...or likes to think she is."

The chief sobered immediately. "This stalker's getting to her?"

"Some, though she'd never admit it."

"Doubt she would. Any idea who's responsible?"

"A couple of theories, but nothing strong enough to haul anyone in."

"My gut says to pull her. Put her on a plane to Hawaii or somewhere as far away from Red Rock as I can get her until we figure out what's going on."

"She won't leave."

"No. She's not one to run from trouble. Would rather meet it square in the face and spit in its eye." He reached for his phone. "I'll put a surveillance on her house."

"I think it would be better if we keep this just between us, Chief. The fewer people who know about this, the better."

The chief drew back his hand. "Are you suggesting that someone on the force is stalking her?"

"At this point, I'm not sure. Technically, only police personnel have access to that cell phone number, but you never know what these hackers can achieve. I've got some leads to follow up on. If any of them pan out, I'll let you know."

"What about Andi? I want her protected."

"I'm looking out for her. Nobody's going to hurt her."

The chief narrowed an eye at Gabe, considering. "All right," he finally agreed. "I'll let you handle this your way, but I'm warning you. If she so much as stubs her toe, I'll personally strip you of your badge, then start on your hide."

Gabe rose. "I'll keep her safe, sir. You have my word."

The chief rose, too. "Whatever you need, it's yours. Nobody messes with one of mine and gets away with it."

"Dudley Harris—that wife beater she put away—is out on parole. I need an address. And I want a copy of Andi's phone records. Both home and her cell. I'd request it myself, but I don't want to take a chance on her getting wind of it. I figure you can pull some strings without her ever being the wiser."

"Consider it done."

Gabe turned for the door, then stopped. "Oh, and, Chief? Don't let on to Andi that you know anything about this. She'd have my hide if she knew I talked to you."

Andi glanced at the clock on the dash as she waited for the traffic light to turn green, and muttered a curse under her breath—8:15. She couldn't believe she'd overslept. In the nine years she'd worked for the department, she'd never once reported in late.

It was Gabe's fault, she decided, tapping her fingers impatiently against the steering wheel. If he hadn't kept her awake half the night with his Goldilocks-search for a comfortable bed to sleep in, she wouldn't have overslept.

She narrowed an eye at the light. She was going to give him a piece of her mind when she saw him.

And leaving the house without waking her was just one more irritation to add to a growing list of grievances against him.

A motor revved in the lane next to her. She ignored it the first time, but when it revved a second time, higher, she shot the driver of the car an exasperated look. She froze, when her gaze struck that of the man in the passenger seat. His eyes were black as Satan's and filled with hate, and could belong to only one man. *Dudley Harris.*

A horn sounded behind her, and she whipped her gaze to the rearview mirror, then up at the light. Noting that it was green, she flipped on the directional signal and made a quick right turn. She glanced in the rearview mirror again and watched as the beat-up sedan passed slowly beneath the light. Dudley stuck his arm out the window, his hand shaped like a gun, and mouthed the word *bang.*

Gabe glanced up as Andi entered the station, then tensed when he saw her face. He quickly stood and crossed the room to intercept her. "What's wrong?"

She kept walking, refusing to meet his gaze. "Nothing. I'm late."

He caught her elbow and spun her around, heading her back out the door.

"Would you stop!" she cried. "I'm late enough as it is."

"So you'll be a little bit later." Once outside, he guided her to a bench beneath a tree and forced her down. "What's wrong? And don't tell me nothing. You're as white as a sheet."

She set her jaw and looked away. "I just saw an old friend. Dudley Harris."

He slammed a fist against his thigh and swore. "Dammit. I knew I shouldn't have left you there alone."

She shot him a scowl. "Yeah, I was meaning to talk to you about that. You could've at least reset the alarm."

He hunkered in front of her. "Did he come to the house?"

"No. He was parked next to me at a red light."

"Did he threaten you?"

She wrapped her arms around her middle and turned away. "No."

"He must've said or done something. You wouldn't be this upset about just seeing the jerk."

She held out her arms. "Do I look upset?" Before he could answer, she rose and pushed past him. "The only thing I am is mad."

He fell into step with her. "At me or Dudley?"

She shot him a scowl. "Both. You made me late for work."

"Me? What did I do?"

"You kept me up half the night traipsing around my house, then you turned off the alarm without bothering to wake me up."

"I thought you could use the rest."

She spun to face him. "*I'll* decide when I need rest. I don't need you or anybody else making my decisions for me."

"Okay," he said and turned away. "Tomorrow morning I'll make sure I reset the alarm for you."

She stared, then stalked after him. "You're not staying with me again, Thunderhawk."

He opened the door to the station and held it for her to pass through first. "Fine. Then we'll spend the night at my place."

She opened her mouth, then slammed it shut as Reynolds passed by on his way out, hiding a smile.

She burned Gabe with a look. "Thanks a lot. Now Reynolds thinks we're sleeping together."

"Look on the bright side," he said, urging her through the entrance. "If he thinks you're sleeping with me, maybe he'll quit asking you out."

Leo gripped the arms of his recliner and strained to peer around Andi. "I thought you were going to bring Thunderhawk with you the next time you came for a visit."

"Very funny, Leo," she said dryly as she dragged up a stool to sit at her former partner's feet.

"So how did the date go?"

"It wasn't a date. It was an assignment."

"Then how did the *assignment* go?"

She dropped her shoulders in disgust. "Can we please talk about something besides Gabe Thunderhawk? I've had about all of him that I can take for a while."

"Okay. Any new developments on the Lost Fortune case?"

She held up a hand. "I don't want to talk about that, either. Too depressing."

"What *do* you want to talk about?"

"Tell me what your doctor said at your appointment this morning."

He flattened his lips. "I don't want to talk about it."

She sat up in alarm. "Have you had a setback? You've been taking your medicine, haven't you? And watching your diet?"

"Yes, I've been taking my medicine and watching my diet. And, no, I haven't had a setback."

She pressed her palm against her heart, relieved. "Then what's the problem?"

"If you can pick and choose what you want to talk about, then so can I. And I *don't* want to talk about my health."

"Fair enough. Pick a topic, then."

He gave her a pat on the head. "Thanks for visiting. Come back again soon."

She looked at him in confusion. "I'm not leaving. I just got here."

He shrugged. "The only things I'm interested in discussing are the cases you're working on and your sex life. Since you're not willing to talk about either of those things, I don't see much point in you hanging around."

"Okay," she said grudgingly. "There are no new developments in the Lost Fortune case. We thought we had a lead in New Orleans, but it turned out to be a dead end."

"New Orleans?"

"Yeah. We found an article in a New Orleans newspaper that mentioned a missing person with a crown-shaped mark on his hip."

"And you went there to check it out?"

"Wasted two days traveling for nothing. Turned out the mark was a tattoo, not a birthmark."

"What hotel did you and Gabe stay in?"

"At the—" She clamped her mouth shut and frowned at him. "Nice try, but your little trick didn't work."

Smug, Leo pushed back in his recliner. "Yeah, it did. So how was it?"

"How was *what?*"

"The sex."

Her mouth fell open. "Leo!"

He tipped his head back and hooted a laugh.

"Judging by the shade of red your face turned, I'd say it must've been good."

She dropped her face to her knees. "You're sick. Really sick."

He leaned over to ruffle her hair. "Ah, come on, Andi. This is Leo you're talking to. Your partner. I knew the minute you walked in the door that you'd done the big one."

She lifted her head to stare at him in horror. "It shows?"

He pushed back in his recliner. "Only to someone who knows you as well as I do. So, how was it?"

She lowered her gaze and plucked at a loose thread on the recliner. "Good. Too good."

"Hell, there's no such thing as 'too good.' Not when you're talking about sex."

"There is if you don't want to repeat it."

"Why wouldn't you? You're a mature woman. If you enjoy having sex with a man, there's no reason to deny yourself the pleasure." He tilted his head to peer at her. "Unless he's not of the same mind. If that's the case…"

She shook her head. "No. He's fine with it. I'm the one with the problem."

He leaned forward and gathered her hand between his. "Listen to me now. I know about what happened before, and I don't want you holding back 'cause you think it could happen again. You're not the same person you were back then. You were nothing but a young girl with stars in her eyes. You're older now. Wiser."

"I may be older, but I don't know about wiser."

"Do you really think you can avoid pain by living your life alone?" He shook his head sadly. "I hate to tell you this, honey, but you're hurting now. And I'm not talking about Gabe. Going through life alone and refusing to feel anything for anybody has its own kind of pain. Me? I'd rather take what pleasure I can out of life than never know any at all."

Andi tugged at a stubborn weed, then sat back hard on her bottom when the roots suddenly broke free. Near tears, she tossed the weed into the bucket at her side. It wasn't helping. Working in her yard always relaxed her, made her forget about her troubles for a while.

But she couldn't blank out of her mind what Leo had said that afternoon.

Going through life alone and refusing to feel anything for anybody has its own kind of pain.

She rubbed a hand over her heart. Being alone wasn't so bad. She'd lived alone for fifteen years and had never once regretted the choice she'd made. She was happy. She had her job, her house.

I'd rather take what pleasure I can out of life than never know any at all.

"That's because you've got Myrna," she argued

under her breath. Leo didn't know yet what it was like to love and lose. He and Myrna had been married for thirty-seven years. What did he know about loss?

With a sigh, she dragged the back of her hand across her forehead, then pushed back up to her knees to search for another weed.

"Want some help?"

She jumped, then rocked back on her heels to scowl up at Gabe. "Fences were made to keep people out, not as an invitation to climb."

He dropped down to hunker beside her. "I didn't climb your fence. I came through the front door."

She pursed her lips. "I locked the front door."

He reached into his pocket and dangled a key in front of her face. "And I unlocked it."

"Hey! That's my spare key."

"Yep." He palmed it, then slid it back into his pocket. "I found it hanging on the rack in the laundry room this morning. Figured you wouldn't mind me using it, since it would make my coming and going easier on you."

"You're not staying with me, Gabe."

"You know, you really ought to record that. Save you from having to say it all the time." He stood and caught her hand. "Come on. I brought dinner."

At the mention of food, her stomach growled, reminding her that she hadn't eaten that day. "Well, I suppose you can stay long enough to eat since you went to the trouble of bringing food."

He opened the back door. "That's mighty generous of you."

She tipped her nose in the air and sailed past him. "I can be nice when I want to be."

Andi lay in her bed, frowning at the ceiling. She didn't know how he did it. She must've told Gabe a zillion times he wasn't spending the night, yet here he was all snuggled up beside her like he owned the dang bed.

She glanced his way, her frown deepening. It wasn't fair that he could sleep, while every nerve in her body tingled with awareness, keeping her awake. She supposed that didn't say much for her appeal, since he seemed to be sleeping just fine.

In spite of her irritation, a soft smile curved her lips as she looked at him. He was so cute when he was asleep. With his hair all rumpled and his hands folded beneath his cheek, he looked boyish, almost innocent. Unable to resist, she eased to her side and touched a finger to his cheek. He flinched, then settled back with a sigh and gathered her hand to hold against his chest.

She stared at their joined hands, stunned by the emotion that gathered in her throat. It was such a tender gesture, yet one that seemed to come so naturally to him, even in sleep. But then everything seemed natural with Gabe. Even sharing a bed. No matter what position she was in when he crawled into bed with her, he always snuggled up close, curving his body around hers, as if he'd been sleeping with her for years. And he never seemed shy about his nudity. Even their first time together, in the sweat lodge, he had stripped off his clothes without hesitation.

But the oddest thing about him was his ability to sleep with her without becoming aroused. They'd slept together three times—though the time in the sweat lodge was probably more like a nap—and only had sex once. Granted, she had very little experience sleeping with men, but she had to believe that most men would at least try something.

Either he had really strong willpower or he found her totally unappealing.

She had to believe it was the former, not the latter. No one could fake the kind of passion he'd exhibited when they'd made love. She shivered, just thinking about it.

I'd rather take what pleasure I can out of life than never know any at all.

She caught her lower lip between her teeth. Did she dare follow Leo's advice? What if she made the huge mistake of falling in love with Gabe and she was hurt again?

But if she didn't take what pleasure was offered to her, what would she miss out on?

The answer was obvious. Warmth. Companion-
ship. Pleasure. Physical release.

But what if he was no longer interested in having
an affair with her?

Unsure of the answer, she lifted her gaze from
their joined hands to peer at his face.

And found him watching her.

"What's the matter?" he asked softly. "Are you
having trouble sleeping?"

She gulped, nodded.

He released her hand and drew her close, weav-
ing his legs through hers. "Close your eyes," he
whispered and began to stroke his fingers along
her back.

She did as he said, but sleep was the furthest
thing from her mind. All she could think about
was the gentle glide of his fingers over her skin,
the warmth of his body pressed against hers. Slowly
she became aware of his arousal against her thigh.

She opened her eyes and found that he was still
looking at her. "Gabe?"

He snuggled closer. "What?"

"Uh…your…well, I can feel your…"

He laughed softly and planted a kiss on the end
of her nose. "It's impossible to hold you this close
and not get turned on. But don't worry. You're safe
with me."

"Gabe?"

"Hmm?"

"What if I told you I didn't want to be safe?"

His hand stopped in midstroke on her back. "I'd say I was dreaming."

She slipped her hand down to cradle him. "This doesn't feel like a dream to me."

"You've got about five seconds to change your mind," he warned her. "One-one-thousand. Two-one-thousand. Three-one-thousand. Four-one-thousand..."

While he counted, she was sliding her body down the length of his, pressing kisses to his chest, his abdomen, his groin. Just as he reached five, she opened her mouth over his sex.

He jerked convulsively, fisting his hands in her hair, then groaned as she swirled her tongue around the tip.

"Andi," he moaned. "You're killing me."

Taking him in her hand again, she crawled up his chest to straddle him and leaned to press a smile against his mouth. "Was that a complaint?"

He pushed his fingers through her hair and drew back to meet her gaze. "Not even close."

Her smile faded at the intensity in his eyes. "I want you inside me," she whispered as she guided his sex to hers. "I want to feel you inside me."

"Andi. Wake up."

She rolled over and curled into a ball. "No," she whined pitifully.

Chuckling, Gabe swatted her behind. "Rise and shine. We've got places to go and people to see."

She dragged a pillow over her head. "It's Saturday. We don't have to work today."

"I know what day it is."

"Then why are you making me get up?"

"We're going to Houston."

She sat up and blinked at him. "Houston? Why do we have to go to Houston?"

"To visit my family."

She fell back on the bed and dropped the pillow over her face. "Uh-uh. I don't want to meet your family."

"This isn't a parade-the-girlfriend-in-front-of-the-family ordeal, if that's what you're worried about. It's my nephew's first birthday."

"Wish him a happy birthday for me."

He caught her ankle and dragged her from the bed. "You can tell him yourself."

"Why do I have to go?" she cried.

"Because I'm not leaving you here alone." He propped her up on her feet and aimed her toward the bathroom. "If you're not in the kitchen dressed and ready to go in fifteen minutes, I'm—"

"Leaving without me?" she asked hopefully.

He gave her a shove toward the bathroom. "No, you're going, even if I have to hog-tie you and throw you in my truck."

Chapter 7

"Where are the clown and balloons?" Andi whispered to Gabe. "I thought they were prerequisites at a kid's birthday party."

Biting back a smile, he sliced into his pork tenderloin. "What can I say. My family is a bunch of stuffed shirts."

Andi had to agree. Of all the people gathered around the unbelievably long dining room table, she and Gabe were the only ones wearing jeans. Two of his brothers even had on suits. Of course, had she known that the birthday meal was going to be served in a formal dining room and on bone china no less, she might've dressed differently herself.

"Andi, Gabe tells me you're a detective on the Red Rock force."

The question came from Gabe's father, who sat at the head of the table. She forced a polite smile. "Yes, sir. Nine years now."

"Can't imagine why anyone would want to work in law enforcement. Especially a woman. The hours are terrible and the pay not much more than a schoolteacher's salary." His father sent Gabe a pointed look. "We'd hoped Gabe would join the law firm, as his brothers did."

Though Gabe's expression never changed, she sensed the tension in him and assumed this must be a sensitive subject.

"Somebody's got to round up the bad guys," Gabe replied. "How else are all you lawyers going to have anyone to prosecute?"

"I'm not arguing the merits of law enforcement," his father replied. "I merely consider it a waste of your intelligence for you to have chosen that field." He glanced at Andi. "Did you know that Gabe graduated with honors from college? He had his pick of law schools and chose to attend the police academy instead."

"His intelligence isn't being wasted," Andi assured Mr. Thunderhawk. "In fact, Gabe is currently working on several high-profile cases with me as a detective, while my partner is on medical leave."

His father snorted a breath. "I doubt it takes

much intelligence to outwit some street thug who dropped out of school to pursue a life of crime."

Andi wadded her napkin into a ball on her lap. "I beg to differ, Mr. Thunderhawk, but many of the crimes today are committed by people with college degrees. Look at Ted Bundy. He was handsome, charming, articulate and was studying to become a lawyer. I doubt anyone would describe him as a street thug or a high school dropout."

Mr. Thunderhawk dismissed her argument with a wave of his hand. "Bundy was crazy."

"I believe the same thing was said about Picasso, Edison and Einstein," Andi returned. "Yet, look at the contributions they made to the world."

He snorted a laugh and picked up his glass. "I notice that none of your examples was involved in law enforcement."

Gabe scraped back his chair. "On that pleasant note," he said as he reached for Andi's hand, "I believe we'll say our goodbyes."

Now Andi understood the impetus behind Gabe's drive to succeed and rather respected him for it. With a father who constantly berated his choice of career and taunted him with his other sons' successes, he could have just as easily folded under the criticism and become a deadbeat.

But understanding what drove Gabe didn't make

her feel any better about ruining his nephew's first birthday party.

She stole a glance his way. His jaw was hard as steel, his hands clenched around the steering wheel as if it were someone's throat. They were almost home and he hadn't said a word throughout the entire trip. Yet, neither had she.

"Gabe—"

"Don't say it," he snapped, cutting her off.

She frowned. "How do you know what I was going to say?"

"You were going to apologize, and it isn't necessary."

"Yes, it is. I never should have said those things to your father. I ruined your nephew's birthday party."

He shook his head. "You didn't ruin anything. The same argument would've taken place whether you were there or not." He shot a glance her way. "Although, I was really impressed with the Ted Bundy angle." He snorted a laugh. "I bet the old man is still chewing on that one."

Andi found herself smiling, in spite of her guilt. "No offense, but your father is a sanctimonious snob."

"None taken, because he is." He glanced her way again, then reached to haul her across the seat. With his gaze on the road, he draped an arm around her shoulders and hugged her against his side. "Thanks for coming to my defense. You didn't have to do that."

"How could I not? Law enforcement is my profession, too. There was no way I was going to just sit there and let him take potshots at you when the bullets were hitting me, too."

He dropped a kiss on the top of her head. "Don't take it personally. He's so blinded by what he considers my failures, I doubt he even realized he was insulting you, too."

She laid a hand on his thigh. "You're not a failure, Gabe. Don't ever allow your father to make you believe you are."

He drew back to look at her in mock surprise. "Was that actually a compliment I heard coming from the lips of Detective Andrea Matthews?"

She winced. "Have I really been that hard on you?"

"Do bears sh—"

She clamped a hand over his mouth. "Okay. I get the point. But if I've been hard on you, it isn't because I doubt your ability. I just question your methods."

"Methods?" he repeated. "I follow procedure."

"Technically, yes. But teamwork is important, and you seem to prefer working alone."

"If the job gets done, what does it matter if one person accomplishes it or eight?"

She drew in a deep breath, searching for a noncombative explanation. "In the months we've been working together it's never been an issue, but there are times when I need to know that I can count on my partner to cover my back."

"And you don't think you can count on me?"

"I don't know whether I can or not. That's the problem. There have been several times when you struck out on your own and left me hanging."

"We were interviewing people. You weren't in any danger."

"You don't know that. Even the most innocent situation can turn deadly."

Scowling, he withdrew his arm from around her shoulders and returned his hand to the wheel. "Okay. I get your point."

"Dammit!"

"Andi?" Gabe dropped the newspaper he'd just opened and broke into a run. "What's wrong?" he asked as he burst into her bedroom. He skidded to a stop, staring. Her room looked like a cyclone had hit it. The linens on her bed were in shreds, and feathers from the pillows covered every surface and floated around his feet. A knife was buried to its hilt in the center of her mattress.

He slowly turned his gaze to the dresser where Andi stood, her back to him, staring at the mirror. Across its surface was scrawled in red lipstick the word *whore*.

He quickly crossed the room caught her arm, drawing her away. "Pack a bag," he ordered. "We're going to my place."

She jerked free. "I'm not going anywhere."

He grabbed her arm and spun her around to face him. "Think, Andi," he said sternly. "If this was happening to someone else, you wouldn't allow her to stay here. You'd put her somewhere safe. Someplace where this psycho couldn't harm her."

"I'm a detective," she reminded him furiously.

"And a damn good one. But this isn't happening to someone else. It's happening to *you,* and because it is, you're not thinking straight. Now tell me honestly. If this was happening to someone else, what would you tell her to do?"

She glared at him another two seconds, then dropped her chin to her chest. "Leave."

He released her and turned away. "While you pack, I'll put in the call to the station, then take a look around."

After arriving at the cabin, Gabe talked Andi into taking a nap with him, then, as soon as he was sure she was asleep, he snuck out. He didn't wake her to tell her where he planned to go or even that he was leaving. If he had, she would have insisted on going with him.

And this was a job that Gabe intended to handle on his own.

It didn't take him long to track down Dudley Harris. Two phone calls and he was headed to the Oasis, a seedy little bar just outside Red Rock city limits, where he'd learned Dudley hung out.

Gabe stepped inside the Oasis and paused, letting his eyes adjust to the change in light. Smoke hung like a cloud in the room. Beneath it lay the rancid odor of old grease and stale beer. He quickly spotted Dudley at a pool table in the back. He ordered a beer, then strolled back for a chat.

"Hey, Dudley."

Bent over a cue stick, sizing up a shot, Dudley glanced up, then back down. "Whadda ya want?"

"Talk. Seems we have a friend in common."

"And who would that be?" Dudley asked.

"Detective Andrea Matthews."

Scowling, Dudley rammed his cue stick against the cue ball. It cracked against the three ball and sent it spinning into the side pocket. "She ain't no friend of mine," he muttered. "Bitch sent me up for two years."

"Bet that pissed you off."

"Damn right," he said, then narrowed an eye at Gabe. "Who'd you say you were?"

"Didn't. Where were you earlier today?"

"Workin'. Parole officer found me a job at the box factory. Got off at five." His eyes sharpened, then narrowed. "Hey, I know who you are. You're that Indian cop."

Before Dudley had a chance to react, Gabe had him up against the wall with a forearm braced against his throat.

"Who I am doesn't matter," he said through clenched teeth. "That I'm Detective Matthews's friend is what you need to remember. If you so much as look in her direction again, you'll be spitting blood for a week."

Glass broke behind him and Gabe dropped low, then spun, kicking out as he straightened. His boot hit Dudley's pool partner square in the chest and sent him hurtling back, the broken beer bottle he held flying. He whirled to face Dudley again, but was a second too late. Dudley's fist connected with his jaw, and he stumbled back, tasting blood. He gave his head a shake to clear it, then bent at the waist and charged, catching Dudley in the stomach and taking him down.

Out of the corner of his eye, he saw the bartender coming toward him, a bat gripped in his hand. Digging a knee into Dudley's neck, he pulled his badge from his pocket and held it up. "Officer Gabe Thunderhawk," he announced loud enough for everyone in the bar to hear him. "Red Rock Police."

The bartender backed off and Gabe turned his full attention to Dudley.

"Now I'm only going to say this once, so listen close. If I get wind that you've been anywhere near Detective Matthews, I'll have your ass on a bus for Huntsville so fast you'll be in a cell before the warden even knows you're there." He rammed his knee harder against Dudley's throat. "Understand?"

Dudley clawed at Gabe's leg, fighting for air. "Okay," he croaked. "Just get off me."

Slowly coming awake, Andi burrowed close, seeking Gabe's warmth. When she found only cool sheets, she opened her eyes and sat up. "Gabe?" When he didn't answer, she rolled from the bed and headed for the stairs.

"Gabe?" she called as she jogged down the steps. Just as she reached the kitchen, the back door opened and Gabe walked in.

"Where did you—" She stopped and stared, then hurried toward him. "What happened to you?" she cried.

He ducked around her and headed for the sink. "It's nothing." He twisted on the tap, cupped a hand beneath the water, then brought it to his mouth. He rinsed, spit, then let out a sigh as the bloody water washed down the drain.

She snatched up a towel and held it out to him. "Don't tell me nothing, when it's obvious you've been in a fight."

Turning, he braced his hips against the edge of the counter and dragged the towel over his face, wincing when it struck the cut on his jaw. "I went to talk to Dudley Harris," he admitted.

"Why? Did you find something at my house that you didn't tell me about?"

He shook his head. "No, but I wasn't going to wait around for you to get hurt before trying to find who's responsible for this." He shrugged a shoulder. "So I went to talk to Dudley."

"I'd say you did a little more than talk."

He worked his jaw, testing the soreness. "Dudley's not much for conversation. For that matter, neither is his friend."

"You fought *two* men?"

"The friend never got in a blow. He got my attention when he broke his beer bottle. I put him out of commission before he had a chance to use it."

She balled her hands into fist, fighting back tears. "I don't know whether to slug you or hug you."

"Personally, I vote for the hug. I've taken enough punches for one day."

She flung her arms around him and held him tight. "Do you know how foolish that was? How dangerous? You could've been seriously hurt."

He drew back to meet her gaze. "But I wasn't," he reminded her. "I did manage to eliminate one of our suspects, though. Dudley said he was at work today. I checked his story with his supervisor, who verified that Dudley didn't leave work until five."

She moved away, her forehead creased with worry. "If not Dudley, then who?" She shot him a warning look over her shoulder. "And don't say Deirdre. I refuse to believe that she would do anything to hurt me."

He held up his hands. "You're the one who brought up her name. Not me."

She turned to face him, her jaw set in a stubborn line. "Take me home."

"No way."

"I've got to clean up the mess. I should have done it before I left."

He caught her hand and drew her back into his arms. "We can do it tomorrow." He cupped his hands on her buttocks and dipped his face to hers. "Tonight I have other plans for you."

Gabe lay on his side, braced on one elbow. Andi lay on her stomach beside him, her cheek pillowed by her folded hands, her face turned away. The moon was full and streamed through the open window, bathing his bed in a silvery glow.

Pensive, he trailed a finger down her back, from the base of her neck to the tip of her tailbone. "What made you decide to become a detective?"

"My dad was one. And, no," she said before he could ask, "he didn't force me to follow in his footsteps like your father tried to make you do."

She turned her opposite cheek to her hands and smiled softly as if at a fond memory. "My mother died just after I was born, so it was always just Dad and me. I was practically raised at the police station. Everything about it fascinated me. Solving cases seemed like a game. You gather all the pieces of the puzzle, then try to fit them together to find the answer. What about you? Why did you choose law enforcement?"

"It wasn't to spite my father, though you'll never be able to convince him of that." He thought for a moment, then dropped his gaze to hide a smile. "This is probably gonna sound hokey, but I wanted to make a difference. Make the world a safer place to live."

"I don't think that's hokey at all. It's a shame more officers don't feel that way. Some wear the badge for the power it gives them. Others just want the paycheck."

"Yeah," he said sadly. "I know what you mean."

Her eyes brightening, she rolled to her side and propped her head on her hand. "If you had your pick of jobs, what would you choose to do?"

"That's no secret. Detective. Preferably homicide. What about you?"

"Promise you won't laugh?"

"Promise."

"A private investigator."

He rolled to his back and hooted a laugh at the ceiling.

She swatted his chest. "You promised you wouldn't laugh."

"Yeah, but that's before I knew what you were going to say."

"Jerk," she muttered. "See if I ever tell you anything again."

"Sorry," he said and rolled back to his side, trying to hide his amusement. "But when you said private investigator, I immediately envisioned you slumped down in a car in the parking lot of a no-tell-motel, wearing a ball cap and toting a camera with a high-powered zoom."

"Private investigators do other things besides trailing spouses who are having affairs."

He cuddled closer. "Enlighten me."

"For starters, they track down stolen or missing children, investigate personal injury and insurance fraud cases. And they get to pick and choose their cases. Can you imagine what it would be like to focus all your time and energy on *one* case and not fifty? To not have to worry about red tape or expense reports or D.A.'s with an attitude?" She fell back with a dreamy sigh. "That would be heaven. Pure heaven."

Laughing, Gabe dropped a kiss on her mouth. "So why don't you do it?"

She shrugged a shoulder. "I like to eat. P.I.'s don't start out with a steady paycheck, you know. Not unless they tie themselves to a corporation or a group of lawyers. It takes time to build a reputation, to develop a clientele."

"Coward."

She jerked up to a sitting position. "I'm not a coward! I'm a realist."

"Doesn't take much to set you off. Mention the word *coward* and it's like touching a match to a stick of dynamite." When she continued to glare at him, he tugged her back down beside him. "Okay. So I don't think you're a coward. But I do think you ought to give being a P.I. a try. You'll never know if you could make a success of it until you do."

"You're just saying that because you want my job."

"Well, it would create an opening."

She punched him in the stomach.

He choked out a laugh and grabbed her hand before she could punch him again. "It was a joke! I swear."

"Ha-ha," she said dryly.

Growing serious, he curled his fingers around her fist and brought it to his chest. "I want to make detective. I won't deny that. But not if it meant stripping you of the title. Now, Leo, on the other hand…"

She gasped, then punched him again when he started laughing. "That's not funny. I like Leo."

He lifted a brow. "And you don't like me?"

She squirmed, suddenly uncomfortable. "I didn't say that."

"Well, do you or don't you?"

Scowling, she turned her face away. "You're all right, I guess."

Gabe sat opposite Prater's desk. "Entry was gained through a window. The perp used a glass cutter to slice out a pane, then simply stuck a hand inside and unfastened the lock."

"She needs a damn security system. I've told her that before."

"I'll see that she has one installed," Gabe replied dryly, though he and the chief both knew the chances of him accomplishing that were, slim. "I called in the break-in, then took Andi to my place."

"What did they find?"

"Zilch. The knife was taken out of Andi's own kitchen and was used to shred her bed linens. The slashes on the fabric matched the blade. No prints were found on any of it. The lipstick used to write the message was hers, too. Again, no prints."

"There's no such thing as the perfect crime," Prater reminded him. "The guy's got to slip up some time."

Gabe lifted a shoulder. "If he has, we haven't caught it. And believe me, we've gone over everything with a fine-tooth comb."

"I want you sticking close to her. Don't let her out of your sight."

"Don't worry. I don't plan to."

* * *

Andi had never lived with a man before and had never understood why any woman would choose to move in with one when she could just as easily live alone. But she was beginning to see the merits of cohabitation. There was always someone around to talk to. And it was kind of nice having a warm body to snuggle up to at night. She hadn't even considered the benefits of splitting up the chores, but having someone to share the cooking and cleaning duties was a definite bonus.

Sex-on-demand wasn't so bad, either. She'd coined the phrase herself after hearing a commercial for a movie channel on television. If you wanted to watch a movie, you didn't have to go to the theater or drive to the store and rent a DVD or video. You just turned it on. Having Gabe around worked in much the same way.

"What are you smiling about?"

She jumped, then glanced around and was surprised to see that the court proceedings were over and people were filing out of the courtroom. "Nothing." She quickly stood. "Guess we're done, huh?"

Prater stood, too, and led the way out. "Looks that way. The lawyers will present their closing arguments tomorrow, then it'll be up to the jury."

They'd given their testimony, which she hoped helped the prosecutor's case. "Let's hope they decide in favor of the state. McPherson deserves a

nice long vacation away from women and temptation."

"Amen to that."

Prater opened the door, then followed her outside
into the sunlight. "You and Gabe getting along all
right?" he asked.

Andi tensed. "Yeah. Why?"

He shrugged a shoulder and started down the
steps. "You living alone so long, I figured you
might have a tough time adjusting to living with a
man."

Stunned, Andi stared. "You know that I've been
staying with Gabe?"

"Yep."

She jogged down the steps to catch up. "But…
how?"

"Gabe told me. He also mentioned the trouble
you've been having." He gave her a pointed look.
"I would've preferred to hear it from you."

"Uh, yeah…well…" She lowered her gaze.

"Your ride's here."

She glanced up to find Gabe's truck parked in
front of the courthouse and Gabe behind the wheel.

She narrowed an eye. "So it is," she muttered,
then said to the chief, "See you tomorrow," and
headed for Gabe's truck.

She yanked open the door and climbed inside.

"How'd it go?" Gabe asked as he reversed from
the parking space.

She whirled on him. "Why did you tell the chief that I was staying with you?"

He stared, obviously caught off guard, then frowned and pulled the gearshift into Drive. "He wasn't supposed to say anything to you about that."

"Well, he did," she snapped, then balled her hands into fists against her knees to keep from slugging him. "I told you I wanted to handle this on my own."

"Look, Andi," he said patiently, "it's not a sign of weakness to ask for help when you need it."

"I didn't ask for his help *or* yours."

His jaw taut with anger, Gabe whipped the truck to the curb, then spun on the seat to face her. "Dammit, Andi, I care about you, and I'm not going to take a chance on you getting hurt."

She drew back, staring. He *cared* about her? He wasn't supposed to feel anything for her at all! They'd agreed to a physical relationship. Period.

Gulping, she tore her gaze from his. "I—I'm not going to get hurt," she said.

"Damn right, you're not," he muttered as he pulled back into traffic. "Because I'm going to see that you don't."

Later that night Andi lay in bed beside Gabe, unable to sleep, her mind whirling with conflicting emotions. It had all started with Gabe's announce-ment that he cared for her. She hadn't admitted it to him, but she'd grown to care for him, too. Worse, she was afraid she was in danger of falling in love with him.

That alone complicated things. But when she added Gabe's desire to make detective to the mix, an already complex situation quickly turned disastrous. Members of the same unit couldn't date or marry. It was against department policy. If Gabe made detective, that meant their relationship would end.

And what if he didn't make detective? What then? Would he be satisfied to continue as a police officer? Or would he seek a detective job on another force, in another city?

Either way spelled disaster for their relationship. It would have to end. There was no other way.

And Andi didn't want it to end.

The next morning Gabe and Andi sat before her computer at the station, searching the national database for missing persons, the same as they had for nearly three months, looking for a match for Lost Fortune.

"This one looks promising," she said, and clicked the link that would reveal a more detailed description of the person.

"How would a guy from Seattle, Washington, end up in a lake in Red Rock, Texas?" Gabe asked doubtfully.

"Weirder things have happened," she reminded him. "Height and weight are close," she said, studying the data listed.

Officer Reynolds stopped at her desk. "Prater wants to see you in his office, Andi."

Without moving her gaze from the screen, she nodded, and scraped back her chair. "It's worth a try," she said to Gabe as she rose. "Give the Seattle police department a call, while I see what the chief wants. I shouldn't be long."

She quickly crossed to the chief's office and stuck her head inside the door. "You wanted to see me?"

He waved her in. "I just got off the phone with the D.A.'s office."

She sank down onto the chair opposite his desk. "And…" she prompted, knowing this had to be about the McPherson case.

"The jury just came in. Took less than an hour to reach a verdict."

The suspense was killing Andi. "Come on, Chief. Spit it out. Are they sending him up or not?"

A smile split his face. "Guilty on both counts. Rape and assault."

Andi went weak with relief. "Thank, God. That's one less pervert on the streets."

"You did a good job. Without the evidence you and Leo gathered, the D.A. wouldn't have had a case."

"Leo's the best."

"He's good," the chief agreed. "Can't argue that. Talked to him last night. Another week and he says his doctor's going to cut him loose."

A knot of dread twisted in Andi's stomach. "I guess that means Gabe will be returning to his regular duties."

"I 'magine so. 'Course, he'll continue to work with you on the Lost Fortune case until it's solved. No sense tryin' to bring Leo up to speed when Gabe's been on the case from the beginning."

When she remained quiet, the chief looked at her curiously. "That's okay with you, isn't it? I can pull him now, if you want me to."

She quickly shook her head and rose. "No. It wouldn't make sense to pull him before the case closes." She turned for the door.

"Had any more trouble from that stalker?"

She stopped in the doorway and glanced back over her shoulder. "No. Maybe he got bored and decided to pick on somebody else for a while."

"I doubt it."

"I can always hope."

He waved her out. "Yeah. Me, too."

She closed the door, then looked toward her desk. Gabe stood beside it with a phone pressed to his ear. Unless she was terribly mistaken, that looked like excitement in his expression. She slowly crossed the room, that knot in her stomach twisting a little tighter. "What's going on?"

He held up a finger, then said into the receiver, "Yes, I will. I appreciate your help." He replaced the receiver, then let out a wild whoop and punched the air with his fists.

She tried to hide her fear with sarcasm. "What? Did you win the lottery or something?"

"Better. That was the detective with the Seattle police department. The report you saw was filed by the guy's girlfriend. She claims he's been missing for three months. And here's the kicker," he went on, oblivious to the fact that he was the only one excited about the news. "The guy has a crown-shaped birthmark on his hip."

Chapter 8

Gabe unlocked the door to the hotel room, then stepped aside, letting Andi enter first. "You're awfully quiet," he said, as he followed her in. "Something bothering you?"

She avoided his gaze, knowing there was no way she could tell him that, if the woman they'd flown to Seattle to meet identified the Lost Fortune body, he would be returning to his duties as an officer. It would break his heart.

She shook her head. "Just tired, I guess."

He dropped his bag on the bed. "How can you be tired? I feel like I could run a twenty-six-mile marathon and still have energy to burn."

She forced a smile, determined not to spoil his excitement at the possibility of closing the case. "I don't know about running a marathon, but I bet I could find the energy to walk down to the pier for some fresh seafood."

He took her bag and tossed it to the bed on top of his, then grabbed her hand. "That's my girl."

By the time they finished eating and strolling through the market, darkness had settled over the pier. With energy still to burn, Gabe suggested a walk along the bay. More relaxed now, Andi agreed.

She stopped and pinched off a piece of bread she'd purchased at the market and tossed it out into the water. She watched as gulls dived to retrieve it. "Did you see that?" she asked Gabe, laughing. "The little one got it." She tore off another chunk and threw it farther out.

"He got it again!" she cried in delight.

"He's smart," Gabe replied.

"Cagey," she corrected, then looped her arm through his and walked on. "He's learned he has to be cunning in order to survive. Brains versus brawn. Brains will win every time."

"Is this the voice of experience speaking?"

She shrugged. "Most of the perps I go up against are bigger than me. If it came to a fight and I had to rely on physical strength alone, I'd probably lose. I have to outsmart them."

"And if you find yourself facing a perp that has brawn and brains, then what?"

She hid a smile. "Then I run like hell."

He dropped back his head and laughed. "I can't see you running from anything."

"I may be stubborn, but I'm not stupid. I know when to back off."

He slung an arm around her shoulders and dropped a kiss on top of her head. "I hope so."

The gesture was so easy, so casual, and a form of affection he'd used often over the past few weeks. So, why did she have the sudden urge to cry?

She blinked rapidly and turned her face away, not wanting him to see the emotion. But she obviously wasn't fast enough.

He stopped and pulled her around to face him. "Why don't you just tell me what's bothering you? And don't say it's nothing," he warned. "I know better."

She wanted to distract him with a sarcastic comeback. But she couldn't seem to work up the strength needed to make it convincing.

"Leo's coming back to work next week."

He stared at her in puzzlement for a moment, then muttered a curse and turned to brace his hands on the railing, glaring out at the water. "And you won't need a partner any longer."

"Not once Leo's back. You'll continue to work on the Fortune case," she assured him. "Prater says it doesn't make sense to pull you when you've been on it from the beginning."

He dropped his head between his arms, obviously realizing what she'd already ascertained.

"So tomorrow could be my last day as a detective."

She wanted to touch him. Place a hand on his back and tell him she was sorry. Instead, she curled her hand into a fist at her side. "It looks that way."

He lifted his head and stared out at the bay and the long stream of silver the moon cast on the water's surface. "How long have you known about this?"

"Since yesterday. Prater told me when he called me into his office."

"And you didn't say anything?"

She heard the resentment in his voice and figured he was entitled. She'd probably feel the same way. "You were pumped about the prospect of closing the Fortune case. I didn't want to ruin that for you."

He stared out at the water a moment longer, then blew out a long breath. Turning, he caught her hand. "Let's go back to the hotel. I'm tired."

Later that night Gabe reached for her in the darkness and held her for what seemed like hours, before slowly making love to her. There was a sadness in his touch, as if he realized, too, that their time together was coming to an end.

The girlfriend who had placed the missing person report was Delilah Johnson, a librarian. A thin woman, with short, mousy-brown hair, she had a fragility that made a person want to protect her.

And Andi was about to break her heart.

She scooted to the edge of her chair, eager to get this over with.

"The man you reported as missing," she began.

"Christopher Jamison," Delilah said, then dabbed a tissue to already red-rimmed eyes. "His name is Christopher Jamison."

"Christopher Jamison," Andi repeated, understanding the woman's need to use the man's name. "You said that Christopher has been missing for three months."

"Yes. About that. He said he was going to Texas."

"Why did you wait three months to file a missing person report? He was your boyfriend. I'd think you would've been more concerned about his safety."

She balled the tissue in her hand. "I loved Christopher."

"Then why wait so long to report him missing?"

"Because I didn't *know* he was missing," she said angrily, then buried her face in her hands.

"I'm sorry," Andi said quietly. "But the questions are necessary in order for us to establish that the man we found is your boyfriend."

Delilah lifted her head and sniffed, nodding. "I know. I just can't bear to think that Christopher might be dead."

"I understand. Take your time."

Delilah took a deep breath, then slowly released it. "I spent the summer in Europe. It was a trip I'd arranged before Christopher and I started dating. I offered to cancel my plans, but he insisted that I go. He said he wouldn't be in Seattle, anyway, as he planned to spend his summer break in Texas. It seemed foolish to cancel, if he wasn't going to be here." She lifted her hands helplessly. "So I went to Europe."

"Did you have any contact with him while you were away?" Andi asked.

"Yes. At first. We e-mailed back and forth almost daily."

"You said 'at first,'" Andi said. "Why did you stop e-mailing him?"

"I didn't," she replied, then dropped her chin. "When several weeks passed without a response from him, I thought perhaps he'd met someone else and it was his way of ending our relationship."

Andi recognized the woman's embarrassment and suspected that the librarian suffered from a low self-esteem. Not wanting to cause her any more discomfort, she opted to focus her questions away from the e-mails.

"When did you return from Europe?" she asked.

"Last week. Late Thursday evening."

"And did you try to contact Christopher then?"

She nodded. "I felt I deserved an explanation of some sort. When I didn't reach him at his home, I didn't consider that something might've happened to him. I assumed he was still out of town."

"When did you suspect that he was missing?"

"Monday. School starts soon and the teachers have mandatory meetings they are required to attend prior to it opening."

"Did you check with the school?"

She nodded tearfully. "They hadn't heard from him, either."

"What about family? Does he have any siblings?"

"A father and two brothers."

"Have you talked to them?"

"I called his father. Mr. Jamison hasn't heard from him, either."

"What about his brothers?" Andi asked.

"I don't know how to get in contact with either of them. Christopher has been estranged from them for years. Emmett, the oldest, joined the FBI shortly after graduating from college. I remember Christopher saying something about him suffering some kind of an emotional breakdown after capturing a serial killer."

"And the younger brother?" Andi prodded.

"Jason." Delilah shrugged. "I don't know anything about him, other than that he broke off contact with his family years ago."

Andi had seen examples of dysfunctional families before, but Christopher Jamison's took the cake.

She decided to change tactics and go for the one answer that would confirm that Christopher was their floater. "You mentioned that Christopher has a crown-shaped birthmark on his hip."

"Yes." Delilah angled her body and placed a hand against her hip. "Right here. He said it was a family trait."

Andi exchanged a look with Gabe, then turned back to Delilah. "The man we found has that same birthmark."

Delilah clapped her hands to her mouth, tears flooding her eyes. "Oh, God. He's dead, then. My Christopher is dead."

"We won't know that for sure until you identify the body."

Her eyes widened in horror. "Oh, no. Please. I can't."

"I'm sorry, Delilah, but someone has to make a positive identification."

"Christopher's father," she said. "He can do it."

"Would you like for us to call him?"

She hesitated, obviously tempted, then shook her head. "No. I should be the one to call him. He shouldn't have to hear about Christopher's death from strangers."

Chief Prater moved up beside Andi, who stood before the two-way window, watching as the medical examiner pulled out the drawer containing the body of Lost Fortune. Gabe had volunteered to go in with Christopher's father, while he made the identification, and stood beside Jamison and opposite the M.E.

"Good thing the Johnson woman knew how to get a hold of her boyfriend's father," Prater said in a low voice. "Seeing her boyfriend like this could give her nightmares for years."

Andi nodded gravely, then stole a glance at Delilah, who sat in a chair across the room, her face buried in her hands. "I'm afraid she's going to have them anyway. This whole thing is too weird."

"Ryan Fortune thinks so, too. I talked to him earlier. Knowing the dead man has the same birthmark as him seems to have thrown him for a loop."

"I imagine it would, when it's supposedly an inherited family trait."

"He wants to talk to Christopher's father. Think Jamison would be willing to meet with him?"

Andi lifted a shoulder. "I can ask."

She tensed as the medical examiner lifted the sheet from Lost Fortune's face. Blake Jamison took one look and his knees buckled. Gabe tightened his hold on the man and leaned to whisper something in his ear. At Jamison's nod, Gabe lifted his head and looked straight at Andi. Though he couldn't see her through the two-way glass, she could see him, and the message he sent was loud and clear.

"Jamison ID'd him," Andi said with a weary sigh. "Our Lost Fortune finally has a name."

Andi and Blake Jamison waited while Gabe approached the reception desk at Fortune TX, Ltd. "We're here to see Ryan Fortune."

"Your name?" the receptionist asked.

"Gabe Thunderhawk, Red Rock Police. Mr. Fortune is expecting us."

She gestured to a grouping of plush chairs. "If you'd like to have a seat, I'll let Mr. Fortune know you're here."

Gabe ushered Andi and Blake Jamison to the sitting area, but Ryan appeared before they had a chance to sit down.

"Mr. Fortune," Gabe said, and shook Ryan's hand. He drew Jamison forward. "This is Blake Jamison."

His face creased in sympathy, Ryan clasped Jamison's hand between both of his. "I'm so sorry for your loss, Mr. Jamison."

Jamison's jaw trembled a bit, but he managed to check his emotions. "Thank you. And, please, there's no need for formalities. Blake is fine."

"Blake, then," Ryan said, and opened a hand. "If you don't mind, we can talk in my office."

When Gabe and Andi hung back, Jamison stopped. "You can join us. I have nothing to hide."

"We'll wait for you here," Gabe told him.

Ryan avoided his desk and led Blake to a more casual grouping of chairs in front of the window that overlooked the manicured grounds of Fortune TX, Ltd.

"Please," he said, indicating for Blake to sit down. "I appreciate your willingness to meet with me," he said as he sat opposite him. "I know that today's events must have been very difficult for you."

Blake drew in a long breath, then blew it out. "You have no idea."

Ryan nodded gravely. "I'm sure I don't. I'll make this conversation as brief as possible. I don't know if you are aware of this, but I have a crown-shaped birthmark on my hip the same as your son's."

"Yes. Chief Prater mentioned that you did."

"As far as I know, this unusual birthmark is unique to my family."

"Yes," Blake agreed. "That's true."

Puzzled by his response, Ryan frowned. "Are you saying that your son is a Fortune?"

"No. My son is a Jamison."

Ryan sank back in his chair in frustration, feeling as if Blake was playing a game of cat and mouse with him. "Then how do you explain your son having a birthmark that you yourself have acknowledged as being unique to the Fortunes?"

"I never said the birthmark was unique to the Fortunes. I said it was unique to your family."

Ryan shot to his feet, his face red with fury. "Are you purposefully trying to drive me crazy? The Fortunes *are* my family."

"Your *adopted* family," Blake clarified.

"I wasn't adopted. My father was Kingston Fortune!"

"Kingston *Jamison* Fortune."

Ryan paled as he realized the connection, then dropped his head to his hands. "Oh, my God. Oh, my God." He slowly lifted his head. "I never once considered that possibility. I didn't know anything about my father's heritage. No one did. He seldom even talked about it. He told us only that he was raised by Hobart and Dora Fortune."

"They did raise him. His birth mother, Eliza Wise, gave him to the Fortunes when he was just a baby. His father, Travis Jamison, never knew of his existence. It's a long story and one I'd rather not go into right now, but Travis's sister was aware of

Kingston's birth and planned to tell Travis that he'd fathered a child. Unfortunately, Travis died before she could tell him about his son."

Appearing exhausted, Blake dragged himself to his feet. "If you will forgive me, I really should be leaving. I—I have arrangements to make for my son."

Ryan stood and extended his hand. "I understand. And thank you for meeting with me. I hope that we can talk again in the future."

Blake shook his hand. "Yes. We should."

As Ryan walked with Blake to the door, an idea occurred to him. "The Fortunes are having a reunion next year in May. We've been trying to pull this off for years. We'd be honored if you and your family would join us."

"I don't know," Blake said hesitantly. "Right now I can't think beyond what I need to do today."

Ryan nodded gravely. "I understand. I'll be in touch."

He watched until Blake rejoined Gabe and Detective Matthews in the reception area, then turned back to his office.

"Who was that?"

Ryan stopped and glanced back, then smiled fondly when he saw his cousin Clyde Fortune approaching from the opposite end of the hall. "It's a long story and not one I'm even sure I can explain."

Clyde held up a hand. "If it's bad news, I don't

want to hear it. I've got enough trouble to deal with of my own."

"Trouble?"

"Yes, trouble," Clyde replied. "The female variety. That half-brained sister of mine, Violet, has invited a college friend of hers to stay at my ranch. For a *month,*" he added, then scowled. "What the hell am I supposed to do with a woman for that length of time?"

Chuckling, Ryan gave him a comforting pat on the back. "I'm sure it won't be as bad as you think."

"No," Clyde grumbled as he stalked away. "It'll be worse."

Jason Wilkes stepped into the break room. "Has anyone seen Ryan?" he asked those sitting at the table, sipping coffee. "I heard he was in the building, but he's not in his office."

Mary, the receptionist at the front desk, glanced his way. "He left for home about ten minutes ago to tell Lily the news."

Frowning, Jason stepped farther into the room wondering what would be so important that Ryan would feel the need to run home and tell his wife. "What news?"

"They identified the body of Lost Fortune," Mary replied smugly, obviously enjoying the fact that she knew something he didn't. "His name was

Christopher Jamison. His father and his girlfriend made the positive identification this morning."

It was all Jason could do to keep the shock from his face. Blake Jamison was in town? He quickly turned away, before anyone could see the panic that had seized him. "I'll try to reach Ryan at home," he said, struggling hard to keep the panic from his voice as he left the break room.

Andi knew she should feel bad that Gabe was going to have to go back to police work when Leo returned. But how could she feel bad about something that allowed them to continue to see each other? If he made detective, their relationship would have to end. She knew that meeting on the sly was an option, but that would never work. She wasn't a rule breaker. Even if she were willing to give it a try, the guilt would eat her alive and that would eventually destroy whatever they had together, anyway, so what was the point?

If she cared for Gabe, truly cared for him, she should want him to be happy...and therein lay the problem. She did care for Gabe. But his happiness—at least in terms of his career—spelled doom for their relationship. He wanted to make detective. It was his goal. His dream. A dream he'd shared with her while they were lying together in bed. But how could she want happiness for him, when that meant giving him up?

She glanced across the squad room at Gabe, who sat at his desk, updating a file. To anyone else, he probably appeared normal. Focused. Busy. But she knew him well enough to recognize the signs of disappointment, of defeat. The slight slump of his shoulders. The tension at one corner of his mouth. The hand he dragged repeatedly through his hair.

Firming her jaw in determination, she pushed back her chair and crossed to Chief Prater's office and peered around his door. "Chief? Could I talk to you for a minute?"

He glanced up from the work spread over his desk, then reared back in his chair and motioned her in. "What's up?"

She closed the door, then took the seat opposite his desk. "It's about Gabe," she began hesitantly.

"What about him?"

"You're aware that he wants to make detective?"

He nodded. "I have his application on file."

She hesitated, unsure how much to say, how far to push. "After working with him on the Lost Fortune case, I can vouch for his abilities. He'd make a good detective. He needs a little work on the concept of teamwork," she admitted, "but that's something he'll gain with more experience in the field."

He looked at her curiously. "Have you fallen for this guy?"

Andi stiffened. "What makes you ask that?"

"You've worked for me for nine years and this

is the first time you've ever campaigned for a co-worker."

She shot to her feet. "I'm not campaigning for Gabe," she said defensively. "I worked with him, is all, and thought you'd want my opinion of his ability to handle the job."

He pursed his lips, hiding a smile. "Why, thank you, Andi. I appreciate you taking the time to share your observations with me."

Her cheeks flaming, she whirled for the door. "You're welcome."

Once in the squad room, she glanced uneasily around. Was she really that obvious? If Prater thought she'd fallen for Gabe, then everybody on the force probably assumed the same thing.

It was time to end this, she told herself, and headed for the exit. And the first order of business was moving out of Gabe's house and back into her own.

"What are you doing?"

Andi wasn't prepared for the sound of his voice, the pain it shot through her. She'd hoped to do this alone and be gone before he came home. Setting her jaw, she stuffed the clothes into her bag. "What does it look like I'm doing? I'm packing."

She heard his footsteps as he came up behind her, and stiffened, praying he wouldn't touch her.

If he did, she was afraid she'd never be able to go through with this.

But he didn't touch her. Instead, he began pulling clothes from her bag. "You're not going anywhere. You're staying right here where I can keep an eye on you."

Furious with him for making this harder than it already was, she snatched the clothes from his hand. "I don't need you watching out for me anymore. Whoever was bothering me has obviously backed off. He hasn't done anything in over a week. Not even a hang-up call."

"That doesn't mean you're out of danger."

She zipped the bag and picked it up, then turned to face him. "I live with danger every day. So do you. We're cops. It's a dangerous job." She turned to go and he grabbed her arm, stopping her.

"Andi, I—"

She held her breath, waiting for him to finish, thinking he'd beg her to stay. Tell her that he couldn't live without her. That this was hurting him as badly as it was her.

Instead, he released her arm and turned away.

Gulping back tears, she all but ran for the door and then to her car. She wouldn't cry, she promised herself as she drove back home. Once she started, she was afraid she'd never be able to stop.

Chief Prater seldom singled out anyone on the force for special recognition and had never handed out an award. But the media coverage surrounding the Lost Fortune case and his connection to the Fortune family had heightened public awareness, which in turn had made it necessary for the city to recognize those individuals responsible for closing the case.

At least that was the only reason Andi could come up with when the chief announced Monday morning that she and Gabe would receive plaques in a public ceremony held that afternoon.

By the time she arrived at the courthouse, where the presentations were to be made, every seat was filled, and people stood three-deep around the perimeter of the room. She saw Gabe standing at the front, talking to Ryan Fortune, and quickly looked away. Just seeing him hurt like nothing had ever hurt her before.

"What are you doing back here?" Chief Prater asked, then caught her elbow and herded her ahead of him up the aisle. "There's a chair reserved for you up front." He shoved her next to Gabe. "Y'all have a seat and we'll get this over with."

Andi quickly sat down. Gabe took the seat next to her, while Prater headed for the microphone.

"If I can have your attention, please," he said, then waited until the room grew quiet. "It isn't often that I recognize men and women on my force. To be honest, I don't believe it's necessary to honor an individual for doing something that's considered a

part of his or her job." He glanced over at Gabe and
Andi. "And I'm sure that if you were to ask Officer Thunderhawk and Detective Matthews, you'd
find they feel the same way. They are in law enforcement because they choose to be. Because they
can't imagine doing anything else. They've dedi-
cated their lives to keeping the law in Red Rock and
maintaining the safety of its residents. They don't
expect any special recognition for doing their job,
any more than Ron there," he said, pointing to the
postmaster, "expects any for doing his.

"But the case that Officer Thunderhawk and Detective Matthews closed last week wasn't a normal
case. From the beginning, it presented problems
not usually associated with crime in our town. For
starters, it dealt with murder. Then there was the
problem with evidence. There was virtually nothing
found at the scene for an investigator to work with.
No weapon. No identification found on the body to
provide a name. We were left with a stranger on our
hands. A John Doe.

"At that point, another group of detectives might
have given up, set the file aside and focused their
attention and time on easier cases. Cases with
actual evidence to trace." He gestured to Gabe and
Andi. "Not these two. They bowed their backs and
dug deeper, worked harder. And their persistence
paid off. Thanks to them, our John Doe now has a
name. Christopher Jamison. His family has claimed

his body and taken him home for a burial long over-due."

He paused a moment, then narrowed an eye at the audience. "Two cases, miles apart, were closed simultaneously. A missing person in Seattle, Washington, and a John Doe right here in Red Rock, Texas. The diligent work of two of Red Rock's finest accomplished this feat. Detective Andrea Matthews and Officer Gabe Thunderhawk."

He motioned for Andi and Gabe to join him at the podium. "I consider it a privilege and an honor to award Detective Andrea Matthews and Officer Gabe Thunderhawk with these plaques signifying service above and beyond the call of duty to this community." He handed Andi a plaque and shook her hand, then presented Gabe with his.

Thinking the presentation was over, Gabe and Andi started back to their seats. Prater's voice stopped them.

"Not so fast, you two," he said, and won a spatter of laughter from the audience. "I have one more presentation to make."

He shuffled through the papers on the podium and pulled one free, then addressed the audience again. "Officer Thunderhawk would normally have not worked this case. But due to one of our regular detectives being out on medical leave, Gabe was given a temporary reassignment of duties. And according to Detective Matthews, the primary on the case, he pulled his weight and then some. She's assured me that he can handle the duties of a full-time detective." Smiling, he turned to Gabe and extended his hand. "Congratulations, Detective Thunderhawk."

Andi drew in a shocked breath, stunned by the announcement. But it took a moment for Gabe to realize what the chief had said. When he did, he glanced at Andi, his forehead furrowed in confusion.

She gave him a nudge. "Go on. Take it. You earned it."

Andi groaned at the sound of the doorbell. With her hands slick with floor wax and another half of the hallway to go before she was done with the job, she wasn't in the mood for company. The doorbell chimed again, and she stuffed the rag into the container of wax, grumbling as she heaved herself up from the floor. She winced as her knees refused to straighten, then hobbled to the front door and pushed up to her toes to peer through the peephole. A very contorted image of Gabe's face let her know that her visitor was the last person in the world she wanted to see.

She steeled herself for the confrontation and opened the door. "Well, well, well, if it isn't the newly appointed Detective Gabe Thunderhawk. I figured you'd be flying so high, you wouldn't touch ground for at least another twenty-four hours."

He pointed at his boots. "Lead soles. Guaranteed to keep a man grounded even under the most extreme circumstances."

"So what can I do for you?" she asked, anxious to send him on his way.

"You could start by inviting me in."

She glanced over her shoulder as if he'd caught her in the middle of something really important. "This really isn't a good time," she began, then cried, "Hey!" when he pushed past her.

"This won't take long," he assured her.

Flattening her lips, she slammed the door. "Make sure that it doesn't. I've got things to do."

"I wanted to thank you."

"For what? I didn't do anything."

"You talked to Prater. I don't know what you told him, but whatever it was, it must've convinced him I could handle the job."

"You *earned* the promotion. I had nothing to do with it."

"Do you know how long Prater's had my application? Two years. Now tell me you didn't have anything to do with it."

"So I told him you handled yourself well on the Lost Fortune case. Big deal."

"I miss you, Andi."

She felt her heart melting and scowled. "Get a dog. I hear they make great companions."

He took a step toward her. "I don't want a dog. I want you."

She thrust out a hand. "Don't, Gabe," she warned. "It's over between us."

He caught her hand and pulled her to his chest. "Says who?"

"It's right there in black and white in your policy and procedure manual. Dating among employees within the same unit is prohibited."

"You knew that when you spoke to Prater, yet you recommended me anyway, knowing it would mean the end of our relationship."

"Is there a point to this conversation? If so, I wish you'd hurry up and make it. I've got things to do."

He stared at her a long time, then slowly released her. His hand on the doorknob, he glanced back. "For what's it worth, you're the first woman who's ever dumped me, and the only one I've ever regretted losing."

Andi had known going in that when a relationship ended between co-workers it could make things awkward on the job. She'd even warned Gabe of that danger.

What she hadn't known—or had chosen to ignore—was how much it would hurt.

With Gabe now officially a detective, he was assigned a desk opposite hers, in the area of the squad room the detectives referred to as the pit. The move made it impossible for Andi to avoid seeing him or escape the sound of his voice.

Though she felt his gaze on her several times that morning, she kept her eyes down and focused on her work. She was trying so hard to block Gabe's nearness, she was startled when Reynolds stopped at her desk.

"We just got a call from a female. Says her ex kidnapped her kid. An officer is en route. Thought you'd want to know."

"Who's the responding officer?"

"Jarrod. The rookie."

Andi glanced over at Gabe and found him watching her.

With his gaze on hers, he scraped his keys from his desk and stood. "I'll take it. You'd probably end up killing poor Jarrod."

Chapter 9

Lenny was a thirty-six-year-old man with the mind of an eight-year-old and a dream to become a policeman some day. He was actually already on the payroll of the Red Rock police department, though his job title was janitor, not officer. He'd worked for the department for six years and did everything from sweeping out the jail cells to running errands.

It was an errand that brought him to Andi's desk shortly after Gabe's departure. He had a tendency to sneak up on people, which was why Andi nearly jumped out of her chair when he touched her shoulder.

She pressed a hand against her heart. "Lenny,"

she said, laughing weakly. "You scared the life out of me."

He leaned close to whisper. "I'm on a mission." He tapped the papers. "Top-secret delivery for Gabe."

She bit back a smile. "He's out on a call." She pointed her pen at the edge of her desk. "You can put it there. I'll see that he gets it."

He set the documents on her desk, as if they were a bomb that might go off if not handled with care. "You won't forget, will you?"

Smiling, she shook her head. "You have my word, Lenny. I'll give them to him the minute he returns."

"Okay, then. Bye."

"Bye, Lenny." Chuckling, she returned her attention to the file she was updating. After a moment, her curiosity got the better of her and she glanced at the papers Lenny had left and noticed the cover sheet had FAX printed on it in bold type. Wondering what information Gabe might have requested, she stretched to pick up the papers and flipped to the second page.

"Phone records?" she asked herself with a frown, then glanced at the top of the page to see whose records he had requested. She clamped her jaw when she saw her own name and cell number listed.

"That jerk," she muttered, then scanned the page, noting the report only showed calls received and placed during the month of August. The same month in which her so-called stalker had started hassling her.

Rising, she circled her desk, sat down behind his and began to dig through his drawers. She didn't feel the slightest bit guilty for prying. After all, he had pried first by requesting her records.

She'd about given up on finding anything else when she noticed a file marked "Aerdna," which was Andrea spelled backward. "Really, Gabe," she muttered as she pulled out the file. "You're going to have to quit watching those detective shows on television."

She quickly thumbed through the contents, finding phone records for her house phone and a profile on her neighbor Richard. Curious—and a little more than irritated—she settled back to read Richard's profile. Married and divorced three times. No surprise there. Five years at current address. No outstanding warrants listed, but a shiver chased down her spine when she saw that he'd been arrested once for assault on a woman.

She flipped the pages back to examine the records for her house phone. The list was short, as she would've expected, since very few people had her home number. She recognized her dentist's number and zeroed in on the numbers following it, remembering that she'd received a hang-up call immediately following the call from her dentist.

210-555-3889. She frowned, not recognizing the number, then followed the line Gabe had drawn to the bottom of the page and the handwritten note: "Pay phone in parking lot of grocery store at 8th and Lee streets."

Obviously, he'd traced each number to its source. But he hadn't had a chance to trace those on her cell yet, she realized. She quickly slid the file back into the drawer, then returned to her desk and picked up the fax Lenny had delivered. She quickly flipped the pages, looking for the date that she and Gabe had returned from their dead-end trip to New Orleans. Finding it, she scanned the time of the calls until she located the approximate time she'd received the welcome-home text message. When she did, she stared, unable to believe what she was seeing.

Deirdre had left her the message? But...why?

There was only one way to find out, she told herself and pushed to her feet.

She'd confront Deirdre.

Deirdre stretched her toes to the footboard and her fingers to the headboard, purring like a cat fat on cream. She'd never imagined that sex could be this good. Not just good, she mentally corrected. Fantastic!

Smiling, she rolled to her stomach and propped her chin on her hands. And it was all due to blind luck. Who would've thought that slapping a guy with a traffic ticket for running a red light would lead to three weeks of glorious, spine-tingling sex? She shivered deliciously. And not just any guy. A hunky, handsome guy with brains, no less.

The doorbell rang and she rolled to her side, to frown in the direction of the living room. Who in the world would be ringing her door at this time of day? Everybody she knew was aware she worked nights and slept during the day. With a shrug, she rolled off the bed and pulled on her robe. Probably the paperboy, she told herself as she headed for the door. She'd been so busy, she'd failed to mail her payment.

But when she opened the door, she was startled to find Andi standing on her stoop.

"Well, hey," she said in surprise. "What are you doing here?"

"I need to talk to you."

Puzzled by the angry set of Andi's jaw, she glanced over her shoulder. "This really isn't a good time," she said hesitantly, then looked back at Andi and squinched her nose and grinned. "I've got a man in my shower."

"This won't take long," Andi assured her and pushed her way inside.

"What's going on?" Deirdre said with concern. "You're scaring me."

Andi whirled and thrust a paper in front of Deirdre's face. "Why've you been hassling me, Deirdre? Is it because of Gabe?"

Stunned, Deirdre drew back, pushing Andi's hand from her face. "What are you talking about? I haven't done anything to you."

"Haven't you?" Andi cried angrily, then thrust the paper in Deirdre's face again. "Look at the number underlined in red. That's *your* number, Deirdre. The number of the cell phone you were issued by the department."

"So?" Deirdre said defensively. "Everybody uses their cells to make personal calls. As long as it isn't long distance, what difference does it make?"

"A hell of a lot when they're using their cells to make harassing phone calls."

Deirdre's mouth dropped open. "I beg your pardon, but I've never made a harassing phone call in my life."

"Gabe might argue that with you. He says you've called him at all hours of the day and night."

She clamped her lips together. "So that's what this is all about. The mighty Gabe Thunderhawk." She tossed up a hand. "Okay. So I called him a few times. Where's the harm in that?"

"And you called me. A text message that could easily be considered a threat."

"I did no such thing!"

"And you also spray painted the word *whore* on my garage door."

Deirdre gasped. "Have you lost your mind? I'd never do a thing like that."

"I would."

Andi snapped up her head, then froze, her gaze fixed on the man who stood in the doorway of Deirdre's bedroom. He had a little more gray at the temples, but he looked virtually the same as he had fifteen years ago. "Wesley?"

A slight smile curved his lips. "Hello, Andrea."

Deirdre looked back and forth between the two in confusion. "You know each other?"

He stepped into the living room, never once moving his gaze from Andi's. "Oh, yes. Andrea and I go way back."

Deirdre stared. "But...how?"

"We met when Andrea was in college. I was one of her professors. Her favorite, as I recall," he added.

"Why?" Andi breathed. "Why have you been stalking me?"

"Stalking?" he repeated, then clucked his tongue. "Stalking is such an ugly term. I prefer to think of it as evening the score. You destroyed my life, ruined my career. Why should you be allowed to continue on, unaffected, while I paid the price for our indiscretions?"

Deirdre gaped at Andi. "You had an affair with Wesley? You *slept* with him?"

"Oh, yes," Wesley said before Andi could respond. "Our little Andrea is quite the harlot. She wore me down with her insistence, seduced me with her youth and her charms."

Her face ravaged with tears, Deirdre lunged at Andi, clawing at her face and her eyes. "He's mine," she cried hysterically. "Mine!"

Andi threw up her hands to protect her face, but managed to hook a foot behind Deirdre's leg. She jerked hard and Deirdre fell back against the floor, then curled into a ball, weeping, her robe open, exposing a bare hip.

Shifting her gaze to Wesley, Andi dragged a hand over her cheek, smearing the blood Deirdre had drawn with her nails. "You sick bastard," she grated out. "You used her, didn't you? You used her to get information about me."

"Oh, I used her all right. But not just for the information." He pushed a foot against Deirdre's hip, forcing her onto her back. "She has an insatiable appetite for sex. And, unlike you, she enjoys experimenting with the darker pleasures to be gained from sex."

"Why, you—" Her eyes wild, Deirdre scrambled up, her fingers curled to attack him.

Laughing, he planted a foot against her chest and shoved her roughly back. She stumbled, fighting for balance, then fell, her head striking the coffee table with a sickening crack. She moaned pitifully, then her eyes shuttered closed and her body went limp. A pool of blood slowly formed beneath her head.

Andi had to fight the urge to go to her, knowing that if she did she would only make herself vulnerable to similar treatment from Wesley. In order to help Deirdre, she had to remain focused. Alert. She had to think.

And she had to keep Wesley talking.

"I didn't destroy your life," she said. "You did that to yourself. You knew the university's rules and you chose to ignore them."

"Rules," he repeated with a weary shake of his head. "And why should the punishment meted out for infractions only affect the faculty and not the students involved? Why should you be allowed to walk away unscathed, while I was stripped of my job, my tenure?"

She lifted a shoulder, feigning unconcern. "You were aware of the chance you were taking, as well as the consequences if you were caught."

"How was I to know that your roommate would hold such a grudge?"

Genuinely puzzled, Andi frowned. "Marcy didn't hold a grudge against me. We were friends."

"Not against you, dear. Against me. Marcy and I were lovers before you and I became involved."

Marcy? she thought in dismay. Marcy had warned her against getting involved with Wesley, but it had never occurred to Andi that her roommate's misgivings were learned firsthand.

He laughed in delight, obviously aware of her shock. "How naive you were. I soon grew bored with her, though. A pretty face, but very little upstairs," he said, pointing to his head. "You, on the other hand, stimulated me both sexually and intellectually. Or would have for a while, anyway. Thanks to Marcy, we'll never know, will we?" He smiled smugly. "She paid for tattling, though. Just as you'll pay for destroying my life."

Oh, God, Andi thought. He'd killed Marcy. He'd destroyed their friendship, then killed her. But... when?

Deirdre moaned, but Andi didn't dare look her way. She had to keep Wesley talking until she could think of a way to overpower him. Her gun was in her shoulder holster and hidden by her blazer. But she didn't dare reach for it. He was too close. One false move, and she'd be looking down the barrel of her own gun. He was fast and he was strong, evidenced by the muscles that corded on his bare chest and arms.

"I'm curious," she said. "How did you persuade Deirdre to help you? She's a cop, as well as my friend. I wouldn't think you'd be able to persuade her to do anything illegal or harmful."

He sputtered a laugh. "You forgot to mention 'dumb.' She never even realized I was using her.

Milking her for information was a piece of cake. Stroke her in the right places and she babbles like a brook."

"What about the text message I received? Did you send that?"

"Of course I did. Deirdre is rather careless with her equipment. Leaves it lying around all the time. While she was in the shower, I borrowed her cell phone. The bitch was never the wiser."

"And the day you embellished my garage door with your unique artwork. How did you know I was at Gabe's?"

"I followed you." He wagged his head, as if disappointed in her. "Really, Andrea. Did you never pay attention in class? Always remain cognizant of your surroundings. I preached that day after day after day." He chuckled, as if at some private joke. "Of course, you were a bit distracted that day, weren't you? All you could think of was getting to that Indian's house and screwing his brains out."

His hand arced out so fast, Andi didn't have time to dodge the blow. It struck her full on the cheek and sent her reeling back.

"Bitch," he muttered and grabbed her by the hair, yanking hard. "Nothing but a whoring bitch."

The second blow hit her opposite cheek and rattled her teeth. Knowing she had only herself to depend on for survival, she grabbed his arm with both hands and lifted her knee, ramming it against his crotch.

Gabe dropped his keys on his desk and glanced over at Reynolds. "Where's Andi?"

"Beats me. I went to the restroom and when I came back she was gone. Maybe she took an early lunch."

Gabe glanced at his watch. "A little early for that." With a shrug, he sat down at his desk and re-opened the file he'd been working on earlier.

"Heard you made detective."

Gabe glanced up and sputtered a laugh when he saw Lenny standing less than three feet away. "I'm going to get bells for your shoes, Lenny."

Lenny edged closer. "I'm practicing sneaking up on criminals."

"Well, you're doing a good job. I never even knew you were there."

"Did you get the papers?"

Gabe flipped a page to make a notation. "What papers?"

"The ones I gave Detective Andi to give you." He laid a hand on the edge of Andi's desk. "I put 'em right here."

Gabe shook his head. "Didn't see any papers."

"But she promised. She said she would give 'em to you when you got back."

Quickly losing his patience, Gabe set aside his pen. "I'm sure she'll give them to me when she returns."

Lenny wrung his hands, clearly upset. "But I promised Marge I would give them to you personally. It was my mission."

Frowning, Gabe asked, "What kind of papers were they?"

"A fax. Marge said they were for your eyes only."

Gabe shot to his feet. "And you gave the papers to Andi?"

His eyes wide in fear, Lenny backed up. "You weren't here. Detective Andi said she'd give them to you."

Realizing that he was scaring the man, Gabe forced himself to calm down. "It's okay, Lenny. It's not your fault. Where's Marge?"

"In her office. I just saw her. She's in a bad mood. She yelled at me."

Gabe ran for the hallway, praying Andi hadn't found something on the fax that identified her stalker and decided to confront the person on her own. He ducked into Marge's office. "The fax you asked Lenny to give me," he said breathlessly. "Can you get me a copy of it?"

"Get in line," she said sourly. "I've got about forty requests ahead of yours."

He slapped his hands down on her desk and shoved his face up in hers. "I *am* the line."

She drew back, eyeing him warily. "Well sure, Gabe. I'll get right on it."

Deirdre.

Gabe had told Andi all along that he suspected Deirdre was the one behind her trouble. But even with the evidence lying on the seat beside him he was having a hard time believing it. She was definitely strange. And possessive. Maybe even a bit vindictive. But he'd never thought her stupid. And only a stupid person would use her own police-issued phone to place a threatening call.

And that made him wonder if there was someone else behind all this. Someone else pushing the buttons and setting Deirdre up to take the fall.

With that in mind, he approached the door to Deirdre's apartment with caution. Standing with his back against the wall, he drew his gun from his holster and listened. At first he heard nothing beyond the sound of traffic on the street behind him. Then he heard it. The muffled sound of voices. One female. One male. He was too far away to be sure, but believed the voices were coming from the bedroom and not the living room.

To his left was the living room window and he leaned closer, trying to see through the gap where the drapes met. Nothing. They were closed too tightly. But as he started to turn back to the door, he noticed a wider gap at the bottom.

Dropping to his knees, he crawled closer to peer through the space. His heart seemed to stop a moment when he saw a woman lying on the floor. Blood pooled beneath a swirl of blond hair. Deirdre. Not Andi. Shamed by the sense of relief he felt, he crawled back to stand by the door, mentally plotting his moves. Kick in the door and leap inside. Feint to the left, in case whoever was in there with Andi had a gun.

Beyond that he'd have to rely on his gut.

Taking a deep breath, he rammed his boot hard against the door. The jam gave with a splintering of wood. He ducked inside and feinted to the left, holding his gun in both hands out in front of him. He quickly scanned the room, but it was empty, except for Deirdre, who remained on the floor, still as death.

He quickly moved to the hallway, then flattened his back against the wall, peering intently into the dark bedroom. Hearing no sound, he eased closer to the door. Keeping the gun aimed at the center of the room, he released one hand to flip on the light and quickly stepped to the left.

As the light blazed on, he saw Andi standing in front of him, her eyes wide, her mouth clamped by the hand of the man who held her as a shield in front of him. The long blade of the hunting knife he held at her throat caught the light and gleamed wickedly.

"Well, hello, Detective Thunderhawk. So glad you could join us."

The man's voice was deceptively calm, but Gabe heard the madness beneath it.

He kept the gun pointed between the man's eyes and slowly eased around the room, trying to get a clear shot. "I'm afraid you have the advantage. You know my name, but I don't know yours."

"Wesley Gardner. *Professor* Wesley Gardner." He lifted a brow. "Perhaps Andrea told you about me?"

Though Andi had confessed to having an affair with a professor, she hadn't offered a name. But even if she had, Gabe wouldn't have given the man the pleasure of knowing he'd left any kind of impression on Andi at all. "Sorry. I don't recall her ever mentioning you."

Wesley stroked the blade along Andi's neck. "Why, Andrea," he scolded. "Surely you didn't try to make Detective Thunderhawk believe you were a virgin? Not when I had the pleasure of removing that particular stigma."

Gabe had heard about all he was willing to listen to. "Let her go," he ordered.

Smiling, Wesley turned the blade at her throat, pricking the skin and drawing a thin line of blood. "I don't think so. Not yet, anyway."

"If you don't let her go, I'll blow your brains out."

The professor chuckled. "You won't chance a shot. Not when you might hit our darling Andrea." He skimmed the blade through the blood, smearing it down her neck. "Unless you want me to slice her pretty little throat, I suggest you drop the gun."

Gabe caught a flicker of movement out of the corner of his eye. *Deirdre.* She was alive and coming down the hallway, a gun in her hand.

It was a chance, a big one, but he didn't believe Deirdre was in on this with Wesley. He released his grip on his gun and let it dangle loosely from his index finger. He saw the panic that widened Andi's eyes, but refused to respond to it.

"You're right, Wesley," he said in defeat and dropped the gun to the floor. "I won't take a chance on Andi getting hurt. I love her too much for that."

He dropped his gaze to Andi. "Partners. Right, Andi? Partner's always cover each other's backs."

He saw her eyes sharpen and knew that she understood what he was trying to telling her.

"Now!" he cried and Andi rammed her foot down on Wesley's instep, then broke free and dived to the floor.

A split second later, a shot ripped the air.

Gabe hit the floor, scooped up his gun, then rolled, covering Andi's body with his own as the shot echoed around and around the room like a volley.

He lifted his head, his gun poised, and saw Wesley crumple to the floor, exposing Deirdre. She stood in the doorway behind him, her hair matted with blood, tears streaming down her face, the gun hanging limp at her side.

Gabe lowered his head to Andi's. "Thank God," he murmured. "Thank God, you're safe."

Uniformed officers moved through the rooms of Deirdre's apartment, dealing with the details associated with any crime scene. But this wasn't any crime scene. This involved one of their own. *Three* of their own, in fact.

As the ambulance attendants pushed the gurney carrying Deirdre through the living room, a tremble shook Andi as she obviously recognized the sound of the wheels rolling across the floor.

Gabe knew he had to get her out of there. She hadn't spoken a word since he'd picked her up from the floor. Hadn't even cried. When the ambulance attendants had attempted to examine her, she'd buried her face against Gabe's neck and clung tighter to him, refusing to let anyone near her.

He caught Chief Prater's eye, then rose, shifting Andi in his arms, and crossed to the door. "We're going to take you to the hospital," he told her, and she clung tighter. "It's okay," he soothed. "I'm not letting you go. Chief Prater will drive us."

Alone in a cubicle of the emergency room, Andi lay on a gurney and stared at the ceiling. Trembles shook her body. The shock was beginning to wear off, and images hurtled through her mind like meteors through a night sky. Wesley's eyes, the evil in them, the madness. Deirdre lying sprawled on the floor, unconscious, blood pooling beneath her head. Andi could feel the knife at her neck, taste the fear that had coated her throat.

Marcy, she thought, and gulped back a sob, remembering. All these years she had despised Marcy for what she'd done to her, to Wesley. She'd blamed her, much the same as Wesley had blamed Marcy, for destroying her life, for robbing her of Wesley. But now she saw that Marcy hadn't been trying to hurt her when she'd informed the university of Andi and Wesley's affair. She'd been trying to protect her. She'd already been used by Wesley, then discarded like a toy a child had grown bored with. She'd only wanted to save Andi from the same treatment, the same heartbreak.

Oh, God, she thought and squeezed her eyes shut to block the shame. She'd loved him. Like a fool, she'd loved Wesley, grieved for him. Even when he'd left without telling her, she hadn't blamed him.

Instead, she'd placed all the blame on Marcy.

She realized that, even then, Wesley had been evil. He'd used her, much as he had Deirdre. He'd discovered her needs, her pleasures, then used them to get what he'd wanted from her. From Andi, he'd only wanted sex, a stroke for his ego. From

Marcy, he'd probably wanted the same thing. But by the time he'd gotten to Deirdre, his needs had changed, had taken on a violent slant. From Deirdre he'd wanted information, access to Andi's life, her habits, her phone number, her address. And once he had those things, when he was sure he had Andi where he wanted her, he probably would've killed Deirdre, just as Andi was sure he'd killed Marcy. Just as he would've eventually killed her, if not for Deirdre and Gabe.

Tears welled in her eyes as she thought of Gabe. She'd put his life in danger, the same as she had Deirdre's. The same as she had Marcy's. Gabe had said he loved her. When Wesley had taunted him, saying Gabe wouldn't shoot because he wouldn't take a chance on hitting Andi, Gabe had lowered his gun and offered his life in exchange for hers. And all because he loved her.

One person was dead because of her, another critically injured. Could she live with herself if Gabe had been killed, too? Could she bear to live without him?

Suddenly panic-stricken, she sat up, her hand going instinctively to the bandage at her throat. She had to get out of here. Gabe would be coming back soon. He'd want to take her home, care for her. She couldn't let him love her. She couldn't allow herself to love him. The pain was simply too much. More than she could bear.

She slid off the gurney and ripped the hospital gown over her head. Grabbing her clothes, she jerked them on, then peeked out the curtains that formed the cubicle. With no one in sight to stop her, she slipped out and began to run.

Chapter 10

"How does it feel to be back at work?"

Leo took a sip of the coffee Andi had poured for him and lifted a shoulder. "Like putting on an old shoe. Comfortable. Familiar. The bonus is getting away from Myrna's yapping for a while."

Andi sputtered a laugh. "Yeah. Like Myrna yaps."

"The woman's a walking megaphone. By the end of the day, my ears are all but bleeding."

Chuckling, Andi started to refill Leo's cup, but he placed a hand over it. "One's my limit. Doctor's orders."

She winced. "Sorry. I forgot."

He waved away the apology. "If you want to be

sorry about something, try the fifteen-hundred-cal-orie-a-day diet he's got me on. Hell, a bird couldn't live on that amount of food."

"You look like you're surviving."

"A lot you know." Grimacing, he took another swig of his coffee. "So when are you coming back to work?"

Andi picked up her emery board and began to saw on her thumbnail, avoiding his gaze. "I don't know. Soon. I just need some time."

"Can't argue that. Have you been to see Deirdre yet?"

She kept her head down. "No."

"They were going to try to stick her with accessory."

She snapped up her head. "They can't do that! She saved my life."

"Yeah. That's what Gabe told 'em. Went to bat for her, which is what you should've done."

She dropped her gaze again, her cheeks heating in shame. "I would've if I'd known."

"You'd've known if you ever answered your damn phone."

When she didn't say anything, he heaved a sigh. "Gabe asked about you."

She sawed harder at her nail. "Tell him I'm fine."

"Said you won't return his calls, either."

She dropped the emery board and snatched up the coffee carafe, crossed to the sink and dumped the coffee down the drain. "If I answered the phone every time it rings, I might as well be at work. The whole point in taking some time off is to get away from it all for a while."

"*It* being Gabe, I assume."

She slammed down the carafe on the counter and whirled. "I didn't say that."

"Didn't have to. Reynolds told me that when back-up arrived at Deirdre's apartment you were holding on to Gabe like you were never going to let go. Said Gabe finally had to pick you up and carry you out, just so the lab guys could do their job."

"I was in shock. People in shock display erratic behavior."

"Mmm-hmm."

"And what's *that* supposed to mean?"

"Just trying to pacify you. When a person's in denial, I'm told it's best to just agree with them. Saves setting 'em off."

"I'm not in denial about anything."

"Come on, Andi. This is Leo you're talking to. You might fool everybody else, but you can't fool me. You're in love with the guy! Why won't you admit that?"

"I'm not in love with him!"

"You damn sure are, and you're breaking the poor guy's heart. You held on to him like he was your last hold on life, then, while he's in the waiting room, wringing his hands, you split, leaving him hanging. He's worried sick about you and you won't even talk to him."

"I told you to tell him I'm fine. I just need some time."

"Time for *what?* To build up those defenses again? To come up with some more of those get-lost-sucker lines you're famous for delivering? Grow up, Andi. You can't run from your feelings anymore." Scowling, he pushed out a hand. "Hell, I know that professor did a number on you. But so what? Lots of people get dumped on before they find the perfect match."

She racked her brain for an argument. "I'm older than Gabe."

"And you consider that a problem? Hell, Myrna threatens to trade me in for a younger model every other day."

"I think you're forgetting department policy. Gabe's a detective now. Officers in the same unit aren't allowed to date or marry."

"Screw department policy."

"Are you suggesting that I ignore the rules?"

"I'm not suggesting you ignore anything. Hell, if you love the guy, get another job! Better yet, stay home and make babies. I've been wanting a grandbaby to bounce on my knee."

Andi clapped her hands over her ears. "I'm not listening to you anymore. Please leave."

Leo heaved himself to his feet. "Hell, I need to

go home anyway. Myrna's liable to set the hounds on me if I'm late for dinner on my first day back at work."

He stooped and bussed a kiss on her cheek. "Think about it, kid," he said, and ruffled her hair. "You're not getting any younger."

Andi flipped open her eyes, instantly awake. She strained to listen, sure that it was a noise that had awakened her.

You're being paranoid, she told herself, and closed her eyes. Wesley's dead. There's no one to bother you anymore. But even with her eyes closed, she continued to listen.

The central air unit came on and she flinched, then forced herself to settle. She wouldn't allow herself to be frightened to stay in her own house alone. That would be ridiculous. Childish. No one was going to hurt her.

There was a loud *thump,* a grunt, then a crash.

She sat up straight, her eyes wide, her heart thumping wildly in her chest. She eased her legs over the side of the bed, tiptoed to her dresser and slid her gun out of its holster. Moving as quietly as possible, she crossed to the doorway. She drew in a deep breath, then lunged into the hallway.

"Freeze! I've got a gun. I'll use it."

"Please do," a voice begged. "Put me out of my misery."

She frowned into the darkness. "Gabe?"

There was a heavy sigh. "Yeah, it's me. I think I broke my foot."

She patted the wall for the light switch, flipped it on. Gabe lay on the floor at the entrance to the hallway, his legs tangled with the ladder she'd left there when she'd changed the lightbulb earlier that day.

"What are you doing here?"

He lifted his head to scowl at her. "Would you mind putting the gun away? I was kidding about wanting you to use it."

Unaware that she'd still been pointing the gun at him, she lowered it to her side. "Is your foot really broken?"

"Hell if I know. It hurts like it is."

"You should take your boot off before your foot starts swelling."

He dragged himself to a sitting position and, wincing, brought his leg up to grip his boot. He tugged, then fell back against the floor, panting, his brow beaded in sweat. "Too late."

Andi didn't want to go to him, but she forced herself forward. "Do you want me to get some scissors and cut it off?"

"If you mean the boot, yeah, please."

She hurried to the kitchen and returned with the scissors. "I'm going to move the ladder first, okay?"

He closed his eyes and nodded.

Working quickly, she moved the ladder, propped it against the wall, then dropped to her knees. "I'm going to need to push your pant leg up. If it hurts, just tell me and I'll stop."

He nodded again, but kept his eyes closed. His face was pale and creased with pain. Keeping her touch gentle, she eased his pant leg up over the top of his boot.

"You okay?" she asked hesitantly.

"Hurry up and cut. It's getting tighter. I can feel it."

Steeling herself for the task, she opened the scissors and slipped a blade between his sock and the leather. She began to cut in slow, even strokes.

"Does it hurt?"

"It's killing me. These are my favorite pair of boots."

She shot him a frown. "If you can joke about it, it mustn't hurt too badly."

She made the final snip, then eased the boot over his heel. Wincing at the size of his swollen ankle, she said, "Maybe I should call an ambulance."

"Get me some ice. Then we'll see."

She returned to the kitchen and came back with a plastic bag filled with ice. "This is going to be cold," she warned.

He sucked in a breath, tensing as she laid the bag across his upper foot.

"Sorry," she murmured.

He caught her hand and tugged her back to sit at his side. "Me, too."

She looked at him in puzzlement. "You're the one who's hurt. Not me."

He opened his eyes and looked at her. "You're hurting, too, Andi. Maybe not your foot. But you're hurting."

She gulped back tears at the compassion in his eyes, knowing he was referring to what had happened at Deirdre's. "I'm okay. I just needed a few days."

"You've had a few days. Every one of 'em felt like a damn year."

She blinked hard to see him through the moisture that filled her eyes. "For me, too."

"You wouldn't talk to me."

"I couldn't. Not then."

"Can you now?"

She nodded, gulped again. "I think so."

He laced his fingers through hers. "Doesn't look like I'm going to be going anywhere for a while, so take your time."

Smiling tearfully, she squeezed his hand. "It had nothing to do with you, Gabe. It was me." She dropped her gaze and swiped a hand across her cheek. "It took me some time to figure that out. With a little help from Leo," she added wryly.

"I knew I liked that guy."

She grimaced. "He knows what buttons to push,

that's for sure. He asked me if I'd been to see Deirdre and why I wouldn't return your phone calls."

"Did you tell him?"

"I couldn't. I don't think I even realized why until later, after he'd left."

"How about enlightening me?"

"I couldn't talk to Deirdre. What would I say to her? Apologizing for all that had happened seemed inadequate or cruel. I don't know which. And I couldn't thank her for saving my life when she had to kill the man she claimed to love in order to save me." She lifted a shoulder. "So I avoided her. The same as I did you."

"Now we're getting to the interesting part. Why wouldn't you talk to me?"

She hitched a breath. "Because it hurt too much," she said tearfully. "You could've been killed because of me."

"Hey, now." He hooked an arm around her neck and pulled her head down to his chest. "We live with danger every day. It's our job. Isn't that what you told me?"

"Y-yes. But this is different."

"Why? Because I was in danger and not just you? Come on, Andi. You can do better than that."

She pushed herself up from his chest. "I love you. Okay? How could I live with myself if something had happened to you and it was my fault?"

"We'll get to that in a minute. First, back up to that first thing you said and say it again."

"I love you?"

"Yeah. That."

She choked a watery laugh. "I do love you. I didn't want to and I'm still not sure that I should."

"But you do," he said cautiously.

"Yeah, I do."

He puffed his cheeks and blew out a shaky breath. "Okay. Now that we've got that settled, let's discuss that other part. About me being hurt and it being your fault. That's not possible, so you have no worries there."

"But it is possible!" she cried. "Wesley could have killed you!"

"And I could have broken my damn neck on that stupid ladder. Would that have been your fault, too?"

"Yes. I was the one who left it there."

"But *I* was the one who tripped over it. And while sneaking into your house, I might add. That was *my* fault, not yours. I make my own decisions, and because I do, I take full responsibility for whatever consequences may occur as a result. Next?"

"Next, what?"

"Next problem."

"That was it."

"So now you'll marry me?"

Her eyes rounded. "Marry you?"

"Yeah. You love me, I love you. We get married and live happily ever after."

Though she'd never allowed herself to think beyond the possibility of simply being with Gabe, the idea of becoming his wife settled over her like a warm cloak.

"I just thought of another problem." She held thumb and finger before his face. "Just a small one."

He heaved a frustrated sigh. "What?"

"We work in the same unit."

"Not a problem. I'll go back to being a police officer."

She looked at him in awe. "You'd do that for me? You'd give up detective so that we could be together?"

"There's a choice?"

"Well, yeah. I could give up detective."

"You were there first. It's only fair that I step down."

"Or I could open my own business. I've always wanted to be a P.I. With a husband to support me, I could afford to take the chance."

He narrowed an eye. "Is that why you're agreeing to marry me?"

Laughing, she bent to kiss him. "That among others."

He wrapped his arms around her and held her close. "Like what?"

"Let's get you to the hospital and get your foot taken care of, then I'll show you."

When she attempted to shift off him, he tightened his grip.

"What?" she asked in confusion.

"I just wanted to tell you I love you. I never thought I'd feel that way about a woman. You proved me wrong."

A shiver chased down her spine at the love she found in his eyes, the warmth. "I love you, too, Gabe. I'm only beginning to realize how much."

Bouquets of flowers and baskets of ivy covered every flat surface in Deirdre's hospital room. Mylar balloons bearing get-well wishes bobbed on long, colorful strings tied to the back of a chair. Greeting cards of every description were taped to the vanity mirror and the wall above her bed.

In spite of the outpouring of love, Deirdre lay with her face turned toward the draped window, her eyes dull, her expression despondent.

Andi hesitated in the doorway, unsure of her welcome.

Gabe gave her nudge. "Go on," he whispered. "I'll be right here outside the door."

Taking a deep breath, she crossed to the bed.

"Hey, Deirdre," she said softly. "How are you feeling?"

Deirdre slowly turned her face to Andi. Tears

filled her eyes. "I'm so sorry. I didn't know. I swear I didn't know."

"Shh," Andi soothed, stroking a hand over her hair. "You don't have anything to apologize for."

"He was going to kill you."

"But he didn't," Andi reminded her. "Thanks to you, I'm still alive."

"How can you say that, after all that he did to you?"

"Because *he* did it, Deirdre. Not you. He used you, just like he used me."

Hoping to tease a smile from her friend, she stroked a finger down her cheek. "You're going to have to give me the name of your hairdresser."

Hitching a breath, Deirdre touched a cautious hand to her hair. "It's hideous, isn't it? They had to shave part of my head when they put in the stitches."

"Might start a new trend. Although I think I've seen punk rockers with similar 'dos."

Deirdre smiled through her tears. "I can't believe you can joke around after what you went through."

"I'm a survivor. Both of us are." She caught Deirdre's hand and gave it a squeeze. "So when are you going to break out of this joint?"

"Monday, I think. My parents are coming to get me. They're going to take me to Houston with them for a while."

"Good idea. But don't let them try to talk you

into moving back home. Red Rock needs you." She squeezed Deirdre's hand again and smiled. "And so do I."

"Anybody got a pen?"

Andi and Deirdre both glanced toward the door.

Deirdre's eyes widened when she saw Gabe there, propped up on crutches, his foot in a cast. "What happened to you?"

Using his newly acquired skill, he swung himself into the room. "Andi got mad at me and broke my foot. Wanna sign my cast?"

Laughing, she struggled to sit up. "Tell me the truth. What really happened?"

"He tripped over a ladder while trying to break into my house," Andi explained.

Deirdre gave them both an exasperated look. "Would one of you please tell me how he broke his foot?"

Gabe slung an arm around Andi's shoulder. "She was telling the truth. I did trip over a ladder while trying to break into her house. What she didn't tell you was that I was breaking in to propose."

Deirdre's eyes rounded. "You're getting married?"

Andi nodded.

"When?"

Andi glanced at Gabe and smiled. "We haven't set a date yet." She looked back at Deirdre. "But I'm hoping you'll agree to be my maid of honor."

"Me?" Deirdre asked, as if shocked that Andi would ask her.

"Sure. You're my best friend. So, will you?"

"Of course I will!" Deirdre cried, then laughed. "Maybe I'll even catch the bouquet."

* * * * *

FAMOUS FAMILIES

YES! Please send me the *Famous Families* collection featuring the Fortunes, the Bravos, the McCabes and the Cavanaughs. This collection will begin with 3 FREE BOOKS and 2 FREE GIFTS in my very first shipment— and more valuable free gifts will follow! My books will arrive in 8 monthly shipments until I have the entire 51-book *Famous Families* collection. I will receive 2-3 free books in each shipment and I will pay just $4.49 U.S./$5.39 CDN for each of the other 4 books in each shipment, plus $2.99 for shipping and handling.* If I decide to keep the entire collection, I'll only have paid for 32 books because 19 books are free. I understand that accepting the 3 free books and gifts places me under no obligation to buy anything. I can always return a shipment and cancel at any time. My free books and gifts are mine to keep no matter what I decide.

268 HCN 9971   468 HCN 9971

Name _____ (PLEASE PRINT) _____

Address _____ Apt. # _____

City _____ State/Prov. _____ Zip/Postal Code _____

Signature (if under 18, a parent or guardian must sign)

Mail to the **Reader Service:**

IN U.S.A.: P.O. Box 1867, Buffalo, NY 14240-1867
IN CANADA: P.O. Box 609, Fort Erie, Ontario L2A 5X3

FFBPA11